Only We Know

By the same author

coming 2 gt u
The Bex Factor
Silenced
Firewallers
Trust Games

Only We Know

Simon Packham

Piccadilly
PRESS

First published in Great Britain in 2015 by Piccadilly Press
Northburgh House, 10 Northburgh Street, London EC1V 0AT

Copyright © Simon Packham 2015

A CIP catalogue record for this book is available
from the British Library.

ISBN: 978-1-84812-427-1

1 3 5 7 9 10 8 6 4 2

Types ... Book Production Limited, ... irk, Stirlingshire

Printed and bound by Clays Ltd, ... Plc

www.piccadilly... .....

Piccadilly Press is part of the Bonnier Publishing Group

For Nick and Francesca

SEPTEMBER

There are three dates in the school calendar that I find particularly loathsome: Valentine's Day, for obvious reasons, April Fool's Day (ditto) and the first morning of the Autumn term, when we must exchange the inspirational pursuits of summer for the dehumanising rituals of a new school year.

Dido's Lament: 1,000 Things I Hate About School

1

EGG ON HIS FACE

The fridge looks all wrong in this tiny kitchen, as if a family of giants has moved in. And there's only room for two at the breakfast bar, so Tilda has taken her Crunchy Nut cornflakes into the lounge and stretched out in front of that new TV channel that only runs repeats of game shows.

My sister isn't best pleased by the whole situation. It's safe to say that moving to a rubbish house in the most boring town on earth was not on Tilda's to-do list. Plus, the new uniform looks crap on her too. So I'm not exactly amazed that she totally blanks me when I smile at her through the serving hatch.

'You need to eat something, Lauren. How about I fix you a milkshake?' says Mum.

'No thanks,' I say, pushing a plate of burnt bacon across the fake marble. 'I feel a bit sick actually.'

The worry lines on Mum's face form an intricate pattern of First World War trenches. 'You don't have to go today if you don't want to, my love. We could always leave it until next week.'

'No, it's not that. It's . . . you know.'

Dad's not a great fan of 'girlie talk'. To save him his blushes, I fix her in the eye and nod at my nether regions. 'I still get slightly . . . nauseous.'

'Of course,' says Mum, obviously angry with herself for not picking up on it. 'I'll fetch you a glass of water.'

Dad downs the rest of his coffee and looks up from his mobile. I know he loves me, but I sometimes think he'd have more luck finding the lost city of Atlantis than suitable subjects for conversations with his eldest daughter.

'I see Arsenal are looking for a new keeper, Lauren. That Ukrainian guy is a good shot-stopper, but he can't kick a dead ball to save his life.'

'Is that right, Dad?'

'Yeah, well, he's a —'

'There's your water, love,' says Mum, flashing Dad a dirty look as she whips away the charred remains of his omelette. 'Now, Lauren, are you *sure* you're ready for this?'

According to my sister, slag bags and rucksacks are in. But from what I've read of the online prospectus, St Thomas's Community College isn't exactly the fashion capital of Europe, so I've chucked the least flattering PE kit in history and a couple of ballpoints into my Beatles messenger bag and hoped for the best. 'Yes, Mum. Ready as I'll ever be.'

'I'll get the car started,' says Dad. 'Come on, Tilda, turn that rubbish off and get a move on.'

'What? No,' I say, the image of turning up for my first day in Year Eleven with an overanxious parent in tow already scarring my imaginary future. 'Thanks, Dad, but I think we're going to walk.'

'Are you sure about that? Wouldn't it be better if I ran you up there at the last minute?'

'No. I'd rather take my time if that's okay. And anyway, shouldn't you have left, like, hours ago?'

'I thought I'd go in late this morning. I wanted to make sure you got there okay.'

'I'll be fine, Dad, promise. And the walk will do us good.'

'Is that right?' says Tilda, who has a talent for creeping into rooms without anyone noticing. 'How do you know I don't want a lift?'

'I just thought —' Surely turning up with Daddy for your first day in Year Ten isn't the greatest look either. 'Well, you don't mind walking, do you, Tilds?'

My sister thinks for a moment. A relieved smile flits briefly across her face. 'Yeah, all right. It might be for the best actually.'

'I suppose I should get off to work then,' says Dad, wincing as he frees himself from the breakfast bar and pecks Mum on the cheek. 'Bye, Nikki. I'll call you at about four, just to see how —'

'Right,' says Mum. I'll text you if anything . . .'

Dad nods. It's a one-hundred-and-fifty-mile round trip to the office these days, and his dodgy back is suffering already. I can see the pain in his eyes as he turns towards me. 'So, this is it then.'

'Yes, Dad.'

'I'd just like you to know that . . .'

There's egg on his face. The question is, do I tell him? 'Dad, I think you might have some —'

But he obviously wants to make a speech. 'I'd just like you to know that, well, we're all really proud of you, Lauren.'

'Thanks, Dad.'

'I know things have been . . . difficult,' he says, plunging his hands into his trouser pockets. 'But . . . with any luck, the worst part is over now. Let's concentrate on the future, shall we?'

Mum is tearing up. 'Your father's right. You've got to get out there and go for it.'

Dad winces again, but this time it's probably down to Mum's weakness for 'inspirational' advertising slogans and not his back. 'Now as far as I'm concerned, you've got nothing to apologise for.' He takes out his Statue of Liberty key ring and starts passing it from one hand to the other. 'But we talked about keeping a low profile, didn't we? Maybe that's the way to go for now. Just promise you won't do anything silly.'

'Yes, Dad, I promise.'

He hasn't kissed me since I was, like, ten years old,

so I should probably point out what a big deal it is when he bends down and plants his lips on the top of my head. 'I'll see you later then, Lauren. I hope it all goes . . . Have a great day. You too, Tilda . . . and look after your sister.'

Well, that was awkward. He tries so hard to say all the right things – and I love him for it. The trouble is, after Dad's little pep talk I'm even more terrified than I was before.

'Right, let's get going then, shall we?' says Tilda. 'I want to have a snoop around before lessons start.'

'Wait,' says Mum, handing me a plastic container and a carton of juice. 'I made you some sandwiches, Lauren. I've put some money on your ParentPay account so you can have lunch in the canteen if you feel up to it. But if you don't want to eat with everyone else, I'm sure you'll be able to find a quiet corner somewhere.'

'What about me?' says Tilda.

'You'll want to eat in the canteen, won't you?' says Mum. 'It'll give you a chance to make new friends.'

'I quite liked the old ones,' murmurs Tilda.

Mum pretends not to hear. 'Well, I must say, you both look . . . lovely.'

'We look like complete dicks,' says Tilda.

'Tilds's right,' I say. 'It's about the worst colour ever. And this polyester skirt is . . . urghh.'

'You should have worn trousers like me then, shouldn't you?' says Tilda.

Mum reaches ominously for her phone. 'Well, I think you look really nice,' she says. 'So how about a quick snap of my two gorgeous girls?'

Enthusiasm levels in the Wilson household reach an all-time low.

'Come on, Lauren, go and stand next to your sister.'

I inch reluctantly towards Tilda. We face the firing squad without a smile between us.

Mum points and shoots anyway. 'Lovely.'

'Well, that's that then,' I say, taking a polite glance at our grim faces on the photo Mum flashes at me. 'Let's get this show on the road.'

'About time too,' says Tilda.

Mum just about holds it together until we reach the front door, where she choreographs the three of us into a tearful group hug. 'Look after each other, won't you, girls?'

'Yes, Mum.'

'Now don't forget, Lauren. You've got a meeting first thing with the Student Welfare guy. Mr . . . Catchpole, is it? He's actually very . . . professional.'

'I won't forget, Mum.'

'And if anyone asks you any difficult questions, just keep calm and —'

'Carry on?' suggests Tilda sarcastically.

'Something like that,' says Mum, reaching for the front door.

A warm shaft of light floods the dingy hallway. Why

is the first day of the school year always so much sunnier than the summer holidays? Not that I've been out much: just a couple of shopping trips and ten minutes with that doctor who kept calling me Laura.

'Goodbye then, girls,' says Mum.

Old habits die hard. I scan the other side of the road for potential persecutors. Two blue-uniformed girls are enjoying a friendly discussion.

'Give me my fags, you slag.'

'Sod off, Ella, they're mine.'

They don't look particularly threatening, but it's enough to send me scuttling back inside. 'I'm sorry, Mum. I can't.'

'Of course you can, Lauren.'

'I'm not ready, I —'

Tilda yawns. She's heard it all before. 'Are you coming or not?'

'She's coming, aren't you, love?' says Mum.

I take a couple of deep breaths. It's supposed to be relaxing. So why do I feel like I'm going to faint? 'Yes, right . . . I just have to – I need the loo. I'll be two seconds, okay?'

2

LOCKED IN THE LAVATORY (PART ONE)

The downstairs toilet stinks of bleach. Mum scrubbed it to death when we first moved in, but you can still see where the killer mushrooms were climbing up the wall.

'Are you okay in there?'

I fumble for my mobile. 'Yes, Mum, I'm . . . Two minutes, yeah?'

There are four numbers in my new address book. Big Moe's is top of the list. I just hope he's not too busy form-filling or refereeing fights. All I need is to hear his voice.

Mum's voice is getting higher by the second. 'Are you sure you're all right, Lauren? Why don't you open the door so we can talk properly about this?'

'I'll be out in a minute, promise.'

At last he picks up. 'Hello, stranger.'

His gravelly Scottish greeting has a miraculously calming effect on my racing heart. 'Hi, Big Moe.'

'So today's the day then, is it?'

"Fraid so.'

'I thought it might be. And how's my favourite fashion victim feeling about that?'

I once told him I'd rather die than wear leopard-print jeans and he's never let me forget it. 'The uniform's a disaster for a start.'

'You poor wee thing. You'll have me crying in a minute.'

'Thanks, Big Moe. You're all heart.'

Actually he really is. So he can't quite conceal his concern when he starts getting serious. 'And what about . . . you know . . . everything else?'

Big Moe's the nearest thing I know to a human lie detector. It's pointless trying to hide it from him. 'I'm scared, Moe, really scared.'

He seems to find that pretty funny. 'Of course you are. It's not rocket science, Lauren.' (What metaphor do you think rocket scientists use? 'It's not GCSE food tech?')

'Who are you talking to in there?' calls Mum.

'No one, I'm just . . .' I lower my voice to an anxious whisper. 'Supposing the same thing happens again, Moe? I don't think I could —'

'It won't,' says Big Moe, almost like he believes it. 'It's different this time.'

'What if one of them's heard about me?'

'I hate to break it to you, Lauren, but you're not exactly a celebrity, you know. And anyway, I hear you're a blonde these days. Your own sister wouldn't recognise you.'

I'm not sure about that, although she sometimes looks

at me like she doesn't know me any more. 'Yeah . . . I suppose.'

'You've worked hard for this, Lauren. If anyone deserves it, it's you.'

'And can I call you if —'

'Of course you can. I'm always here for you, you know that.'

'Thanks, Moe.'

'But you won't need to. You're tough, Lauren; tough as old boots.'

'I don't feel it right now.'

Somewhere in the background a female voice starts kicking off. 'Sorry, got to go,' says Big Moe. 'Now you look after yourself, Lauren. And just remember, there are some people out there who'd like to see you fail. It's up to you to prove them wrong.'

3

UNWILLINGLY TO SCHOOL

A few years back, I had quite a temper on me. Some people said I had 'anger management issues', but I never lost it with my sister.

When Tilds was born, Dad thought I might be jealous of the new baby, so the first time he took me to the hospital to meet her, he bought me a toy police car to keep me quiet. He needn't have bothered, because apparently I loved her right from the start. When she was little we spent hours playing weddings and funerals with her Polly Pockets, and on her first day at primary school I told everyone in her class that if they were mean to my little sister they'd have to fight me. And later on, when we were both getting into fashion, we'd sneak a couple of Mum's magazines up to my bedroom and make these huge collages of our 'winter collections'. In fact, the only thing we ever argued about was hair wax.

All that changed, of course, although I'd kind of hoped that somewhere down the line we'd get back to the way we were. And that's why it hurts so much, the way she looks at me sometimes – the way my name seems to stick in her throat.

But I keep trying. Starting a new school together could be the perfect bonding opportunity.

'You do realise it's the school where that girl ran off with the drama teacher, don't you, Tilds?'

'Where do you think I've been for the last year? In a padded cell?'

'Sorry, I just thought . . .'

We walk in silence as far as the roundabout. That's when I can't pretend any more. Suddenly there are blue uniforms everywhere, joking and laughing and spitting and farting, swearing and kissing and leering and hugging. And they're all headed in one direction – towards the school gates at the top of the hill.

The blood drains from my face as my heart picks up speed. Even the tiniest Year Sevens, with their huge rucksacks and even huger fake smiles, seem to be handling it better than me. Sweating pig-like into my sixty per cent polyester blouse, I scan the conker trees at the side of the road for potential puking spots.

'Are you okay?' says Tilda, sounding suspiciously like she actually cares.

'I don't know.'

'Try not to worry. I'm sure the teachers will be looking out for you.'

'You reckon?'

Come to think of it, Tilda looks pretty scared herself.

'You heard Dad,' she says. 'Keep your head down and you'll be fine.'

It's not exactly the way I imagined it, but right now I'd do almost anything for an easy life. 'I just wish I didn't need to.'

'Yeah, well, you wouldn't have needed to if you hadn't —'

'I'm sorry. None of this is your fault. It's not fair that you've had to —'

'No,' says Tilda.

I move in closer and give her a hug. 'You've changed your perfume, haven't you?'

Tilda pulls away. 'It's a new start for me too, you know. I wanted something more . . . sophisticated.'

'It's nice, suits you.' It may sound like small talk, but believe me this is massive. It feels like we're kind of communicating at last. If we carry on like this, I might get my sister back.

Tilda touches me lightly on the shoulder. 'Look, good luck and everything. I really hope it works out for you. But do you mind if I . . .'

'What is it, Tilds?'

'Do you mind if I walk the rest of the way on my own?'

'Why?' I say, realising immediately what a stupid question it is.

'You know why,' says Tilda.

4

CATCH FORTY-SEVEN AND THREE QUARTERS

I lose sight of Tilda as the school gates swallow her up. She doesn't look back at me, and to be honest, I'd probably start crying if she did. But once I'm safely through the gates myself, the creeping paranoia gets a little less creepy and I calm down for a bit.

I mean, if you believed everything you read online, you'd never get out of bed in the morning, right? Dad self-diagnoses a hundred fatal illnesses a fortnight, but he still manages to drag the bins out every Thursday. And if you saw what they said about St Thomas's Community College, you'd probably lock up your daughters and throw away the key. We're not just talking dodgy drama teachers here. If there's any truth in some of the stuff I've read on Twitter, I'd be better off hiring a couple of bodyguards and a personal tutor – and I certainly wouldn't enlist on any war graves trips.

But so far, it doesn't actually seem that bad. My old

school was really, well, old school – dark gloomy corridors and cold stone floors. This place looks like a cross between a trendy office and a modern art gallery: all rounded corners and windows, with a strange Pokémon-like construction in the middle of the playground and waste-paper bins with special holes for recycling your Coke cans.

Apart from the usual X-rated banter and a boy with personal hygiene issues, the kids don't look that bad either. Tilda was right about Year Eleven hair – the messy bun I took so much trouble creating this morning blends in perfectly. I try to avoid eye contact wherever possible, but the harmless-looking girl I ask for directions to the main reception actually smiles at me. She doesn't even direct me to the bottom of the school field, because after a right past the Learning Resources Centre (which I'm guessing is code for library) and straight on through the double doors, here I am in front of the reception desk.

'Hi, I'm Lauren Wilson. I'm supposed to be seeing the Head of Student Welfare?'

And unlike my old school, where they practically dived for cover whenever they saw me coming, the receptionist greets me like a fanatical holiday rep. 'Hi, Lauren, welcome to St Thomas's.'

'Thank you.'

'You'll find Mr Catchpole next to the boys' toilets. His new office, I mean. Just knock and walk straight in.'

'Right.'

A man in an ailing brown jacket is watering the ailing brown pot plant on top of the filing cabinet. Alongside it is a photograph of a group of kids in front of a war memorial, flanked by a wild-haired woman in knee-length earrings and the man in the ailing brown jacket who appears to be smiling at her.

But the man in the photograph looks about ten years younger than the harassed specimen who turns to face me like an old-style Bond villain.

'Ah . . . Lauren, I've been expecting you.'

'Right.'

'Welcome to St Thomas's.'

'Right . . . thanks.'

'I'm Mr Catchpole – head of Student Welfare. Please, have a seat. Let me just . . .' He takes a pair of bulging files from the Tesco bag on the corner of his desk. 'Now I've read through your notes . . . most of them.'

'Oh.'

'Re-taking Year Eleven at a different school is certainly unusual. Then again, it's fair to say that these are exceptional circumstances.'

'Yes.'

On the wall behind him is a huge poster entitled *Our School Values*. Underneath is a row of random words in bright colours that are supposed to look like they've been scrawled on a whiteboard by a precocious Year Seven, but are almost certainly the work of one of those 'overpaid design consultants' that Dad's always ranting about.

FREEDOM COLLABORATION COURAGE DIVERSITY
CREATIVITY TOLERANCE

Mr Catchpole seems pleased that I'm taking an interest. 'You'll be hearing a lot about values at St Thomas's, Lauren. It's something Mr Edmonds, our head teacher, is very passionate about. Unfortunately he's off sick for at least another month. But you'll find a list in the back of your extended learning record. I suggest you have a good look at them.'

'I will – thanks.'

'I want you to know that we're going to look after you, Lauren. If there's anything you need – catch-up sessions or just a friendly ear, please don't hesitate to ask.'

Underneath the unforgivable brown jacket, he seems like an okay bloke. Although I can't help noticing that both friendly ears are in desperate need of a haircut. 'I won't – thanks.'

'Now, before I send you down to meet your new tutor group, have you got any questions?'

Only one – and I hardly dare ask it. So I stare hopefully at *Freedom*, trying to find the right words. 'Does everyone here . . . know about me? The teachers, I mean.'

Mr Catchpole coughs, grabs one of his friendly ears and starts twiddling. 'We thought it was probably best if the . . . *exact* details of your past were only made available on a need-to-know basis. There's myself and Mr Edmonds, of course, and two members of the senior management team. Other than that, the only other person who's been fully briefed is your form tutor, Miss Hoolyhan.'

'Right.'

'I've deliberately put you in 11CH. Miss Hoolyhan is one of our most experienced teachers. *Should* you have any problems you can always —'

Two sharp knocks at the door put him out of his misery. A girl with virtually no make-up and her hair tied back in a pigtail walks in.

'Ah, Katherine, good,' says Mr Catchpole. 'Katherine's going to be your student mentor. She'll make sure you know where all your lessons are and help you to settle in.'

'It's Katherine with a K,' says the girl with the pigtail.

And I feel like asking if she'll be giving me a spelling test. But the last thing I need is to alienate my student mentor, so I smile politely and try to get her onside. 'Like Kate Middleton you mean?' The thought that she could have anything in common with her royal deliciousness is enough to make me crack a smile.

But not my student mentor. 'Like Katherine Mansfield – the short-story writer.'

'Oh . . . right . . . So what do they call you – Katie or Kate?'

'They don't call me anything.'

'Right.'

'*Any*way,' says Mr Catchpole, taking a last despairing

glance at my notes. 'I'll leave you in Katherine's capable hands.'

If that's a smile, it's not exactly what I'd call reassuring.

'We don't judge people here, Lauren. Life's what you make of it. I'm sure you'll bear that in mind.'

5

THE NEW GIRL

'What was all that about?' says Katherine, ignoring the sniggers that seem to follow her down the corridor.

'How do you mean?'

'The whole tragic backstory bit? You're not one of those kids with cancer, are you?'

'No.'

'So why the special treatment?'

'What special treatment?'

'The breakfast conference with Uncle Colin. Most new kids get two minutes with their form tutor and a map that's not even to scale. What did he say to you anyway?'

'Not a lot. Just some stuff about values.'

'Yes, Catchpole's big on that these days. He knows the value of everything and the price of nothing – totally useless when he's in Tesco.'

If that's supposed to be a joke, I don't get it. 'Yeah, right.'

'But it still doesn't explain why I'm supposed to be babysitting you. Apparently it was Hoolyhan's idea.'

'Well, there you are.'

But the cross-examination continues. 'So what are you doing at St Thomas's? I don't know if you read the newspapers, Lauren, but it's not the type of school that education ministers are queuing up to send their daughters to.'

Luckily it's a question I've been revising for. 'We've just moved into the area. My dad's got a new job. I think it was the only school with a free place.' (The last part is actually true.)

'Yes, well I can believe that,' says Katherine. 'Not exactly brilliant timing though, is it – right in the middle of your GCSEs?'

'I suppose not.'

Paranoia is stalking me again. A school is a school after all, no matter how many recycling bins it's got.

'Are you shaking?' says Katherine. 'Look, I don't mean to be rude, Lauren, but it's not exactly your first day at "big school", is it? Unlike this sorry specimen.'

A Year Seven straggler has been cut off from the herd. He stands beneath the *Are You Getting Your Five a Day?* poster, staring forlornly at a photocopied map.

'What's the problem?' asks Katherine.

'I think I'm lost,' sobs the pathetic Year Seven.

'Where do you need to get to?'

'My tutor base.' He dabs his eyes with his map. 'It's in the science block.'

'I wouldn't let them see you crying if I were you,' says Katherine. 'And anyway, there's nothing to cry about, because you're nearly there. Turn left at the end of the corridor and it's right in front of you.'

He smiles like a lottery winner and starts running. 'Thanks.'

'It does get better you know,' calls Katherine, waiting until he's safely round the corner before adding, 'by about the end of Year Nine.'

A moment later, we stop in front of a blue door.

I reach up and check my hair. 'Is this it then?'

'Yes, this is it,' says Katherine. 'Follow me.'

I try to delay her a few seconds longer. 'What are they like? The other kids I mean.'

'I won't lie to you, Lauren. We're not talking Hogwarts here.'

So what *are* we talking? As the door opens, I prepare myself for the worst. But no one takes much notice as Katherine crosses to the front table and I slip into the seat beside her.

The woman from the photo on Mr Catchpole's filing cabinet is handing out timetables. She's still wearing knee-length earrings, but the bright colours have been replaced by a layer of black. 'Ah, Lauren, how lovely to see you. I'm Miss Hoolyhan, your form tutor.'

'Hello, miss.'

'Mind if I introduce you, Lauren?' she whispers. 'It might be good to get it over with.'

'Okay, fine.'

'You'd better stand up so everyone can see you.'

24

I rise reluctantly, turning to face my new tutor group with soggy armpits and a sickly smile. It might not be the moment of truth exactly, but it's certainly time for the first reality check.

'Listen carefully for a moment,' says Miss Hoolyhan. 'I want you all to say hello to Lauren Wilson.'

They chant it back like mutant zombies, 'Hello, Lauren Wilson.'

Everyone laughs, including Miss Hoolyhan. And so do I, because it's not malicious, just silly. A couple of them are definitely smiling at me and there's even a wolf whistle from the back. Katherine tuts and mutters 'idiot', but considering the doomsday scenarios I've been playing out in my head, it's just an incredible relief.

'Lauren's new to the area,' says Miss Hoolyhan. 'She doesn't know anyone at all round here. So I hope you'll make her welcome.'

'I'll make you welcome, babe,' comes a voice from the back.

'Yes, thank you, Conor,' says Miss Hoolyhan. 'That's quite enough of that.'

Conor obviously doesn't think so. 'Tall, isn't she, miss?'

'I don't see what —'

'Oi, Lauren, do you get dizzy up there?'

My sickly smile gets even sicker.

'You know what they say about tall girls, don't you, miss?'

'No, Conor, I —'

'They've got massive . . .' He wiggles his hands in front of his chest. '. . . feet!'

I close my eyes and wait for the others to join in. But it doesn't happen.

'Give it a rest, Conor,' says a girl with perfect blonde highlights. 'No one thinks you're funny, all right?'

'All I'm saying is, if the lovely Lauren needs someone to hold her hand on her first day then Conor Corcoran's your man.'

Miss Hoolyhan gestures at me to sit down. 'Yes, thank you, Conor. I think we've got that covered.'

'Don't worry about him,' says Katherine. 'He's just the latest in a long dynasty of dickheads. This school's full of them. Believe me, it can only get worse.'

But it really doesn't. Miss Hoolyhan hands out more timetables and our ELRs (we used to call them homework diaries, but they're extended learning records here), and then makes a little speech about not making the wrong choices and starting Year Eleven as you mean to go on.

It's brilliant. No one gives me a second look. And time passes so quickly that I can hardly believe it when the bell goes.

'Just a second, Lauren,' says Miss Hoolyhan. 'Before you charge off, can I have a quick word please?'

'Yes, miss.'

Katherine is lurking like a sinister guide dog.

'Would you mind waiting outside, Katherine? There's something I need to say to Lauren.'

Katherine stands her ground. 'Are you sure about that, miss? I'm the one who's supposed to be looking after her. Wouldn't it be better if you told me too?'

'I don't think so, Katherine. It's only some extra admin anyway. Now if you don't mind, I really do need to crack on.'

Katherine slinks to the door. 'I'll be right outside.'

Miss Hoolyhan clears her throat, shuffles some papers, and generally looks about as comfortable as a teacup in a field of bulls.

Eventually she speaks. 'There's something I feel I ought to mention.'

She wouldn't, would she? I mean she *couldn't*. It's what they decided at all those meetings; that it was better for everyone if certain subjects were strictly off limits.

'We've had some . . . situations at St Thomas's – quite recently actually – where certain students could have come to me with their problems.' She caresses the tassels of her black silk scarf. 'But for various reasons, which I still don't really understand, they chose not to.'

I'm relieved and confused at the same time. 'Oh, I see.'

'What I'm trying to say is that I hope if you have any difficulties – and I really can't see why you should – I want you to feel comfortable talking to me. You would feel comfortable about that, wouldn't you, Lauren?'

'Yes, miss,' I lie.

'We won't judge you here.'

(It seems like everyone judged that girl who ran off with the teacher.)

'I just want to get on with it, miss. Start living my life again.'

'That's a great attitude, Lauren. Now, I think Katherine's waiting for you. Enjoy your first lesson at St Thomas's.'

(She obviously doesn't know what it is.) 'Thanks, miss.'

'Oh and, Lauren . . . ?'

'Yes?'

'I think you're very brave.'

6

LOCKED IN THE LAVATORY (PART TWO)

Girls' changing rooms always smell the same – of toxic body sprays and intimidation. I've had some of the worst times of my life in these places so it's hardly surprising that, in spite of the sweaty atmosphere, it really gives me the shivers.

I sit on the bum-scrunching wooden bench beneath the pegs, praying for an act of God (or at least a fire drill) so that I won't have to start squeezing myself into those horrid Lycra shorts.

It's not that I'm particularly self-conscious or anything, but getting my kit off in front of thirty budding body-image consultants is not my idea of fun. I've been there, done that, got the mental scars, and a couple of real ones to prove it.

'More changing and less yattering please,' says the prison warder in the tracksuit. 'I want you out on the netball courts in two minutes.'

Katherine looks like a fish on a bicycle in her PE kit. 'Oh God, not that. Anything but that.'

'Don't you like netball then?'

'Yes, very funny, Lauren. But if you want to be a comedienne you're going to have to work on your material.'

The prison warder stands over me, her whistle dangling. She obviously doesn't know my 'tragic backstory', so I won't be getting any special treatment. 'Did you not hear me or something? By the time we get out there, it'll be time to pack up again. So get a move on please.'

'Yes, miss.'

I hang my jacket on the peg and take off my tie. But as soon as I start unbuttoning my top, I lose all control of my fingers, and I can't go on.

Meanwhile, Katherine has gone off on a comedy routine of her own. 'Of course, any game where you have to wear bibs is bound to be infantile. And I'll tell you what I *really* hate . . .'

But I never get to find out. My neck is burning, my knees are trembling and my chest feels like it's going to implode. It's been a while now, but I have a pretty good idea what's coming next. I need to get out of here before the tunnel vision kicks in.

'Are you all right?' says Katherine. 'You've gone a very funny colour.'

I grab my Beatles messenger bag and stumble to the cubicles at the back.

One's out of order and the other one's locked. I hammer on the door. 'Open up. Please, please, I need to —'

'All right, all right, I won't be a minute.' A girl with a slag bag emerges. 'Sorry about that, it's like the bloody Niagara Falls down there. Are you on too?'

'Yes,' I lie, pushing past her into the cubicle and locking the door.

Hot flushes give way to cold sweats. And I really think I'm going to die.

Maybe I have already, because when it all goes quiet in the changing room, I hear a voice from the other side.

'What are you doing in there?'

I know it's nearly ending when I almost manage to speak. 'I'm just . . .'

'Look, everyone hates PE,' says Katherine. 'It's a basic human emotion. But it's on the national curriculum, Lauren, so we have to suck it up.'

'Have they all gone yet?'

'Yes. And much as I love talking to lavatory doors, you really need to get changed.'

Panic attack over. My breathing returns to normal and I reach into my messenger bag for those dreaded shorts. 'All right, give me two minutes.'

By the time we get to the netball courts, the girl on her period is handing out bibs. She nods at me like a sister in arms. 'All sorted then?'

'Yeah, thanks.'

'You're tall,' she says. 'You'd better go Goal Attack.' She scowls at Katherine. 'Wing Defence, and try not to get in the way.'

Katherine's still working on her comedy routine as we take our positions. 'What a moronic game. Seven – or is it eight? – girls trying to avoid an inflated piece of plastic. And it's highly sexual you know, Lauren? Balls in holes and all that.'

Katherine doesn't look like an expert on sex. I'd take a bet that her pasty features are as un-kissed by human-kind as they are by the sun. And she's certainly no expert when it comes to netball.

The girl on her period charges about like an advert for sanitary towels. Katherine ambles down the wing, like a tortoise on tranquilisers. The rest of us take a leisurely stroll in the late-summer sun, occasionally shouting 'foot-work' or 'that's an obstruction' to make it look like we care. And when the boys start arriving back from the sports hall, I thank God that it's nearly over.

Talk about bad timing. By some fluke of nature, just as I'm wandering back into the goal circle, the ball magic-ally materialises in my hands.

'Come on,' says the girl on her period. 'Shoot.'

Conor Corcoran presses his face up to the fence. 'Yo, Dizzy, let's see what you've got.'

There's something else you should know about me. I'm actually really good at this game. That's why it's so tempting to plop it straight into the net. But I'll never make that mistake again. That's why I trip and giggle, and let the ball bounce out of play.

Conor Corcoran laughs his spiky-haired dickhead off. 'Talk about throwing like a girl. My nan could do better than that – and she's dead.'

'Shut up, you sexist idiot,' says Katherine. 'Why don't you go back to the Stone Age where you belong?'

There was a time when it would have made me angry too. Conor Corcoran doesn't know how lucky he is.

7

GRAND TOUR

At second break I manage to give Katherine the slip for five minutes, so I can eat my sandwiches in peace. I'm good at finding hiding places, and the stairwell in the art block is perfect. But she sniffs me out in the end, and the next thing I know I'm taking the 'grand tour' with the least enthusiastic tour guide on earth.

'Why, this is hell. Nor am I out of it,' says Katherine. 'But if you really want to know how I feel about the place, you should read my blog.'

'What's it called?'

'*Dido's Lament: 1,000 Things I Hate about School.*'

'Right, yeah, sounds interesting.'

She takes me to all the 'must know' locations. The learning resources centre ('What kind of a brainless bureaucrat wastes all that money on a ridiculous fingerprint system when they don't even have the complete works of Jane Austen?'), the music block ('Hoolyhan means well, but the wind band is worse than water torture'), and the

ICT suite ('Welcome back to the twentieth century').

We end up at the Millennium Pagoda in the playground (or courtyard as they call it here) – a sort of Chinese bandstand with picnic benches in the middle for the 'lonely and talented'. Katherine introduces me to some of her fellow 'endangered species': two chess players and an astronomer, a cellist on a bad hair day and a boy who claims to read fiction for pleasure, 'but never speaks'.

'One day this lot will inherit the earth,' says Katherine, 'but for now, it's the best place to keep away from the others.'

'Where are they anyway?' I say. 'The rest of them. I don't think I've seen anyone from our tutor group.'

'The "ordinaries" you mean?' says Katherine. 'Whenever the sun comes out they have this cow-like weakness for loafing about on the field.'

'Oh right,' I say. 'Can we go and have a look?'

'I don't think so, Lauren. No point trying to run before you can walk – I'm talking metaphorically of course.'

'Okay fine, tomorrow perhaps.'

'*Perhaps*,' says Katherine, exchanging a meaningful glance with the knotty-haired cellist. 'Why not wait until you know what you're up against?'

And the mute fiction-lover nods his wholehearted agreement.

But the rest of the day goes far better than I expected. Although I keep my head down, like Dad told me, that doesn't stop a steady stream of kids from my tutor group coming up to introduce themselves, and when I answer a question in history ('What were the principal conditions of the New Deal?'), the only reaction is a 'Very good, Lauren, but don't forget the Soil Conservation Act.'

In fact, by the time the final bell goes, I'm starting to think that St Thomas's Community College isn't nearly as bad as it's cracked up to be.

8

FRIEND REQUESTS

It's nine o' clock by the time Dad gets home from work, so I have to go through the whole interrogation again.

'And what about the teachers – no problems there, I hope?'

'No, Dad.'

It's supposed to be one of her fasting days, but Mum's already on her second glass of Rioja. 'It couldn't have gone better, Mike. She even answered a question in history.'

'Good,' says Dad, joining us on the sofa with a middle-aged groan. 'Let's hope it carries on that way.'

Tilda is slobbed out in the armchair, one eye on her mobile, the other on *Strike It Lucky*. 'Aren't you going to ask me how *I* got on?'

'Yes of course,' says Dad. 'How did it go, Tilda?'

'Terrible,' she says. 'I told you I'd hate the place.'

'You'll get used to it,' says Dad, pouring himself the remains of the bottle and turning back to me. 'So no one gave you a hard time, Lauren?'

'No, why should they?'

'And you're quite sure you've done nothing to draw attention to yourself?'

He can't leave it alone, can he? 'Look, I'm not hiding in the library all day, if that's what you want.'

Mum puts her arm round me. 'No, love, course not. That's not what we want at all. Is it, Michael?'

Dad shakes his head.

'It's just important that you don't get off on the wrong foot,' says Mum.

'I know that . . . And everything was fine, Mum, I promise.' I grab the iPad and escape into cyberspace.

Dad escapes to his glass of Rioja. 'So come on then, Tilda. What was so terrible about it?'

And you can see them relaxing as my sister tells them about her argument with the maths teacher, and a boy in her tutor group who she thinks is on drugs.

Lucky I didn't tell them about my panic attack. That would have freaked them out for sure. But the thing is, now that I've got the first day over with, I honestly think that school's going to be okay.

And the iPad more or less confirms it. 'Oh wow, that's amazing.'

'What is it, love?' says Mum.

'It's my new Facebook. Guess how many friend requests I've had?'

Mum's face takes a dive. 'I didn't even know you'd created a new account.'

'You thought it was a good idea. Don't you remember?'

'Come on then,' says Tilda. 'How many?'

'Eleven,' I say. 'Not bad for my first day.'

Dad is wrestling with a bag of salt and vinegar crisps. 'It looks like you've made a good first impression then.'

Tilda's obviously desperate to say something. But she doesn't come out with it until Dad follows Mum into the kitchen with the empty glasses.

'No need to look so pleased with yourself.'

'I wasn't.'

'I mean, it's not like they're for real, are they?'

'What?'

'Doesn't matter, forget it.'

'No come on, Tilds, what do you mean?'

'Think about it,' she says. 'Do you honestly believe they'd still want to be friends if they knew what you'd done?'

9

STRANGE MEETING

Day three and I'm starting to wonder what all the fuss was about. The other kids are way friendlier than at my old school (not difficult, it's true), lessons are about as bearable as they could ever be (especially textiles) and by second break I'm so comfortable about the place that I even tell Katherine I'm going out to the field.

'Well, I'm coming with you,' she says. 'Miss Hoolyhan told me to stick to you like superglue.'

She's been doing that all right. 'It's okay, Katherine, why don't you stay and finish your book?'

'It's completely predictable anyway. And the main character's so shallow I feel like slapping her.' She stuffs the offending paperback into her rucksack. 'Come on, you might as well see them in their natural habitat.'

I love the smell of freshly mown grass. And I never thought I'd say this about a field full of eleven- to sixteen-year-olds, but it looks kind of inviting out there

– almost as if the fine weather brings out the best in them.

They certainly look a lot more human without their jackets and ties – laughing and texting, sunbathing and bantering, shoving grass down each others' necks. If you look carefully there's even some sneaky kissing going on – all played out to the sounds of the summer on a tinny orchestra of mobile phones.

It gets better. She keeps saying how much she hates it here, but there's Tilda demonstrating dance moves to some new friends. I raise my hand to wave at her, but she turns away at the last moment and I pretend to be sorting my hair.

Katherine starts on the character assassinations. 'See that lot?'

'The girls from our tutor group, you mean?'

Katherine nods. 'Well, you see the two in the middle?'

'What, the one with the cool creepers and the girl with expensive highlights?'

'How should I know?' says Katherine. 'But if you've got any self-respect, you'll keep away from them.'

'Why, what for?'

'Because Magda and Izzy are all the things that little girls are supposed to aspire to be – pretty, popular and practically perfect. Mind you, I wouldn't mind betting there's an eating disorder or two between them.'

It slips out before I can stop myself. 'Eating disorders aren't funny, you know.'

'Well, a brain tumour then. We live in hope.'

The Year Eleven boys are playing football. Conor Corcoran is hogging the ball in the middle of the park, but he lobs it back to his goalkeeper the moment he sees me. 'Oi, Dizzy, wanna come out with me tonight?'

'Just ignore him,' says Katherine. 'He's like a puppy. Give him any encouragement and he'll be all over you.'

The goalie's worse than that Ukrainian guy Dad keeps on about. He can't kick to save his life. The ball balloons up in the air and bounces towards me on the touchline.

So does Conor. 'Come on, Dizzy. Give it here.'

And without thinking, I kick it back at him as hard as I can.

Conor goes to ground clutching his most intelligent body parts. 'Urghhhhhh.'

I promised Dad I wouldn't do anything silly, but that has to qualify as my dumbest move yet. Except maybe it isn't. Because everyone who witnessed it seems to think it's the funniest thing ever. One boy puts on a high-pitched voice and does castration jokes, I'm pretty sure Magda (or was it Izzy?) just waved at me, and the goalkeeper who can't kick shouts, 'Nice shot, Lauren – right in the balls.'

I know I'm supposed to keep my head down, but I can't help feeling pleased that he remembers my name.

Conor recovers the power of speech. 'Do me a favour. I've seen her throw. At least I know it wasn't on purpose.'

And I'm basking in the adulation that thumping a football into Conor Corcoran's dangly bits obviously inspires when I see something that plunges me back into the dark ages.

Perhaps he's one of the footballers, or maybe he's just come to laugh at Conor, but the fair-haired boy with the Mediterranean tan seems to materialise from out of nowhere.

This time the tunnel vision kicks in almost immediately, as the only person on the school field still wearing a tie bares his teeth and walks slowly towards me.

Oh my God. It can't be.

Back in the dark ages, he wore more make-up than me and his pale face was half hidden behind a jet-black fringe.

But it's the eyes that give him away.

10

LONG TIME NO SEE

'Who's that?' I say.

Even Katherine's voice softens. 'Oh that. That's Harry Heasman. Fancy him, do you?'

'What . . . no . . . course not.'

'Why not?' says Katherine. 'Everyone else does.'

'Even you?'

'I wouldn't go that far. Put it this way, Harry's "good" popular. Not the kind of popular you are when you wear the "right" shoes and only talk to the "right" people – the kind you are from treating everyone the same and being a gentleman.'

H a gentleman? It's not exactly the first description that springs to mind. And now he's so close I can smell him. But it's not the stench of stale Benson & Hedges I'm expecting – more like soap and maybe even a hint of Calvin Klein.

'Hi, I'm Harry,' he says, in a voice about an octave deeper

than the one I remember. 'You're new here, aren't you?'

I can't speak.

Katherine speaks for me. 'This is Lauren, Harry. Guess who's supposed to be looking after her?'

'Nice name,' he says, glancing down at my legs, but pretending not to. 'Suits you.'

At first I think he's trying to mess with my head. It's the sort of thing that H would have found funny.

'And how are you settling in at St Thomas's?'

But I still can't speak.

H speaks for me. 'Takes a bit of getting used to, doesn't it? Don't worry, you'll be fine.'

And suddenly I realise I'm not thinking straight. Okay it's true, I want to believe it more than anything in the world, but actually, when you look at it rationally, it seems like a perfectly reasonable explanation: he doesn't know who I am.

Thank God for that.

But it's H all right, although of course I pretend not to recognise him. The trouble is, 'playing it cool' isn't nearly so easy when you're sweating like a triathlete and you've lost the power of speech.

'You look like you've seen a ghost.' He smiles. 'Are you all right?'

The field starts turning somersaults; my head starts spinning in the opposite direction. But just as I'm surrendering myself to the inevitable sickly blackout, a powerful instinct for self-preservation enables me to stumble my way through half a sentence. 'I've got to go. Miss Hoolyhan said I should . . .'

And I turn on my heels and run.

11

PROFILE PICTURE

I just about keep it together for the rest of the day. Katherine does most of my talking for me anyway, but even she remarks on how quiet I am. And there's a nasty moment when I spot H walking towards us in the corridor. Luckily I have the presence of mind to duck down behind the lockers and pretend I'm looking for my ELR.

The first thing I do when I get home is run upstairs and find him on Facebook. I stare at his profile picture, wondering how a face can have changed so much and yet still be so unmistakable.

It's the one doomsday scenario I've never even considered. There was always a slim chance that someone from my old school might track me down, but I haven't seen H since we were both into Pokémon.

That was four summers ago. We only knew each other for about a month. Unfortunately, that's all it takes. Because the whole idea of moving here was that no one would have a clue about me. What was the point of uprooting my whole family if there's someone at school who already knows?

And what do I do now? Track him down tomorrow and beg him to keep his mouth shut? Supposing he refuses? And even if he does go along with it, what are the chances of him letting something slip by mistake? This time next week it could be all round the school.

Except.

I'm forgetting the one good thing about the whole situation: I'm ninety-nine per cent certain he hasn't recognised me.

And it's not that surprising. H could never hold eye contact. He spent most of the time staring at the floor. Even if he did sneak the occasional glance in my direction, I've changed far more than he has. There's my hair for a start, plus I'm nearly two feet taller and wear make-up now. Like Big Moe said, even my own sister wouldn't recognise me.

Maybe it's not such a big deal after all. If I could just act normally around him, there's no reason he should remember me.

Is there?

That's what I want to believe. The truth is, I've done enough running away to last a lifetime. I like it here. I'm starting to feel almost human at last. Why let one little setback ruin everything? I can do this, I know I can.

And that's the mantra I repeat to myself as I stand in front of the mirror, checking my eyelids for telltale signs of eczema. 'You can do it, you can do it, you can —'

'It's the first sign of madness you know.'

'Eh?'

Mum is standing in the doorway. 'Talking to yourself.'

'Oh, no I was . . .'

'Is everything okay, Lauren? You ran upstairs so quickly we didn't get time for our usual chat.'

'I just wanted to get started on my homework.'

'Really?' says Mum. 'I thought there might be . . . problems.'

'No, no, *no*,' I say, flipping down my laptop before she notices the smiley profile picture. 'It's this textiles project I'm working on. I'm really excited about it.'

'Right,' says Mum, removing a mouldy coffee mug from my bedside table. 'So it's all good then?'

Well, I can't tell her about H, can I? She'd have a fit. I probably shouldn't even mention it to Big Moe. And I'm certainly not telling Tilda – she's scared enough as it is. They say that talking makes things better; sometimes it's more sensible to keep quiet.

'Yes, Mum,' I lie. 'It's all good.'

12

HARRY'S GAME

The next day, I realise how blind I've been. Everywhere you look there are photos of Harry Heasman: standing with the other prefects in the main corridor, part of the victorious basketball team in the sports hall trophy cabinet, and even more surprisingly for someone who witnessed his frequent attempts to murder Arctic Monkeys' songs, if you look carefully at the cast photos of *Oliver!* outside the drama studio, you'll see he makes a pretty convincing Artful Dodger.

It all makes sense now, the stuff he told me about his school: the music teacher who wanted to mother him, the funny-shaped corridors, the mad PSHE guy who always carries a Tesco bag.

But even if I have to keep my distance for the next ten months, I'm still glad to know he's doing okay – *better* than okay. In fact, if you'd told me four summers ago that he'd end up as 'deputy head student' I'd have said you were crazy. And I couldn't help smiling when I saw him chugging up the hill this morning on a little red moped (a 50cc Honda City Express). H was only twelve when I knew him. Back then he wouldn't have been seen dead on that thing, although he would probably have made a pretty good stab at killing himself on it. But if his mode of transport was a touch surprising, it wasn't half as weird as walking into assembly and finding him standing on the stage telling the Year Tens to shut up. *And some of them actually did.*

So by the time I arrive at my first English lesson (can't believe they've put me in the top set) and see H sitting by the window, my heart might skip a beat or two, but at least I don't go into total meltdown mode. And I'm making my way to the spare seat next to Magda and Izzy when a cold vice-like hand grips me by the wrist.

'It's all right, Lauren, I've saved you a place,' says Katherine.

'Oh, thanks.'

'Did you get to maths all right?'

'Yeah, thanks, no problem.'

'Don't worry about the big bad Woolf,' she says, nodding at the woman in the Marks & Spencer suit. 'She's not the worst teacher at St Thomas's. Though I never know why such an obvious stranger to passion thinks she has anything worth saying about the great works of literature.'

'Well, I suppose she . . .'

And that's when I catch a glimpse of the old H. He's taking two ballpoints, a blue paperback, his ELR and an exercise book from his leather messenger bag and laying them out in front of him. Two seconds later he puts them back in his bag. Two seconds after that he lays them out again. The third time he gets it 'right'.

'Are you staring at Harry?' says Katherine. 'I knew you fancied him.'

That girl is too observant for her own good. 'No, it's not that. I —'

'It's all right,' says Katherine. 'If you're going to get passionate about anything, Harry Heasman's a good place to start. Except if you're a teacher, of course. Not that *that* would ever happen.'

Mrs Woolf certainly doesn't look like a man-eater. 'You must be Lauren. Mr Catchpole said you'd be joining us.'

'Yes, miss.'

'You may have covered some of the set works already. But it won't do you any harm to go over them again. What play were you studying?'

'*Romeo and Juliet*, miss.'

There's a sort of collective snigger.

Mrs Woolf licks her lips. 'I'm afraid we're not doing that this year. We decided to look at *Pygmalion* by George Bernard Shaw instead.' She faces the class with a don't-mess-with-me glare. 'So what can any of you tell Lauren about the play?'

'It would make a good musical, miss.'

'And it's got swearing in it.'

The whole class, apart from me and Katherine, recites

the only quotation everyone knows: '*Walk! Not bloody likely. I am going in a taxi.*'

'All right, that's enough,' says Mrs Woolf. 'I expect you know the basic plot, don't you, Lauren?'

'It's the one about the professor guy who turns the flower-girl into a lady, isn't it?'

'Sexist rubbish,' mutters Katherine.

'I tell you what,' says Mrs Woolf, 'why don't we read a bit? Lauren, perhaps you'd like to be Eliza Doolittle – you'll have to share with Katherine, I'm afraid.' She smiles adoringly at the deputy head student. 'Harry, can you read Professor Higgins, please?'

'So what do we think?' says Mrs Woolf. 'Some critics have said that *Pygmalion*'s not about turning a flower-girl into a duchess, but about turning a woman into a human being. Could a person really change like that?'

'It all depends who you're trying to convince, doesn't it?' says Katherine. 'I mean some people are so shallow, they only judge you by your looks.'

'Guilty,' says Magda, pointing at Katherine like she's a witch.

'How about you, Lauren? What do you think?'

I can almost feel the eczema bubbling up on the back of my neck. 'Well, I'm not sure, miss. I suppose if —'

'I think it's possible for someone to change,' says Harry. 'But it's a lot easier if no one knows what you were like in the first place. Like the guests at the embassy dinner

– it's the first time any of them have seen Eliza Doolittle, so they've got no preconceptions.'

'A bit like Lauren, you mean,' says Izzy with a sly smile.

'What are you talking about?' I say, tightening my calves and preparing to be attacked.

Unlike her highlights, Izzy's timing is less than perfect. 'Well, I stalked your Facebook, didn't I?'

'So what?'

'Well, there's nothing on it,' says Izzy, almost like she's taken it as a personal insult. 'No profile picture, no status updates, no nothing.'

'It's my mum,' I say, grabbing the first unlikely explanation that comes into my head. 'She's a bit weird about social networking.'

'What, like that girl with the purity ring?' says Magda. 'She's not even allowed to watch *The Simpsons*.'

'And anyway,' I say, 'Facebook's pretty uncool these days, isn't it?'

Mrs Woolf checks the ceiling for cobwebs. 'I'm not sure I see the relevance of this, Izzy.'

'It's what we do, miss. Even my dad Googles everyone before he meets them. How are we supposed to know what she's like if there's nothing about her online?'

'Because you couldn't possibly try asking her, could you?' says Katherine.

Questions rain down on me from every side:

Are you on Twitter?

What school did you go to?

How tall are you?

KFC or Nando's?

Are you in a relationship?

Is it with a teacher?

Is that why you left your old school?

Battlefield or COD?

But it's not Mrs Woolf who comes to my rescue. It's H.

'Look, if you really want to know about Lauren, I'll tell you, okay?' he says.

Everyone goes quiet. Shit, what's he going to say?

'She's an international drugs dealer, right? So she's hiding out at St Thomas's because the FBI are after her and she's heard how tight security is.'

A few groans, and one enormous sigh of relief.

'Now can we get on, please?' says Mrs Woolf. 'Perhaps we should go through a couple of possible exam questions.'

'Sorry,' whispers Katherine. 'I should have warned you that might happen. Well, at least Harry's got your back.'

That's what's so worrying. Why would he try to protect me like that? I could have coped with their stupid questions (I've been kind of expecting them anyway), but if H has the slightest suspicion about who I am, I really need to know.

13

WORDS TO THE WISE

The fingerprint system in the canteen reminds me of a prison. I'd normally steer well clear of any situations involving large groups of teenagers and food, but Katherine's taken her sandwiches to the Millennium Pagoda, so it seemed like my best chance.

I grab my tray and race towards H, hurdling rucksacks and swerving to avoid the flying sachets of tomato sauce. If I don't bust a gut, someone else will get to him first.

'Is this seat taken?'

'Go for it,' says H.

'Thanks.'

Now that I'm here, I'm not sure what I can say without making him suspicious. So I take a sip of healthy option Slush Puppie and stare into my pasta.

'Sorry about English,' says H. 'That lot can be a right pain. I could have a word if you like.'

'No, *don't*, please. I mean, thanks, but I'd rather you didn't.'

'No worries.' He's the only person in the canteen attacking his panini with a plastic knife and fork. 'It's not bad here you know, Lauren. You'll be all right.'

'Why shouldn't I be all right?'

'No reason. I like people to be happy, that's all.' He sticks his finger down his throat and mimes puking. 'Something like that, anyway.'

The hair really suits him – different, but in a good way. I almost feel like putting it off for a bit and enjoying the moment. Except I'm not here to admire his new hairstyle; the sooner I get this over with, the sooner I can breathe easy again.

'Can I ask you something . . . Harry?'

'Nothing personal, I hope. Whatever they're saying about me, it's not true, okay?' He sees that I'm serious. 'Yeah, sure, what is it?'

'Don't I . . . know you from somewhere?'

He hesitates, swallowing a mouthful of panini before carefully positioning his plastic cutlery on the side of the tray. 'Is that a chat-up line or something, Lauren?'

'No, course not. I just have this funny feeling we might have met before.' I study his face for telltale signs of recognition.

Not a flicker, just the ghost of a seductive smile. 'I think I'd remember a girl like you.'

'Really?'

'You weren't at Glastonbury, were you? My dad took me to see Neil Young.'

'You're not still into him, are you?'

'What do you mean "still"?'

'Nothing. I just didn't think anyone was any more,' I add quickly.

'I take it you weren't there then?' says H.

'No, I think me and my mum were in the States.'

'Oh, right. And what were you doing over there – running from the FBI, I suppose?'

I really shouldn't have mentioned America. 'Oh, you know . . .'

'What, sightseeing and stuff?'

'Yeah, kind of.' One more question and I'll know for sure. 'So . . . Harry?'

'Yes.'

'How do you make an elephant laugh?'

And he stares at me like I'm absolutely mad. So mad that just for a moment he almost seems lost for words. 'What the hell are you talking about?'

He really doesn't remember.

And you know what? A small part of me is actually disappointed.

'Forget it. You must remind me of someone else.'

'Thank goodness for that!' He slings his messenger bag over his shoulder and prepares to leave. His face turns serious for a moment. 'A word to the wise, Lauren.'

'Yes?'

'Whatever you do at St Thomas's, never *ever* touch the spicy sausage pasta. It's like puke in a plastic cup.'

'Oh right. I'll remember that – thanks.'

'Anyway, got to go, Duke of Edinburgh Award meeting. See you around perhaps.'

'Yeah . . . perhaps.'

When he gets to the drinks machine, he turns and smiles at me. And for some reason, I can't help smiling back. But my smile gets even broader when I see who's slipped into the empty seat opposite. I had a nasty feeling she was avoiding me.

'Hi, Tilda, how's it going?'

She opens her pot of pasta and sniffs suspiciously.

'It's not spicy sausage, is it?'

'Yeah, so what?'

'Apparently it's disgusting.'

But my sister's in no mood for small talk. 'No, I'll tell you what's disgusting, shall I?'

'What?'

'You. What do you think you're doing?'

'Having lunch. What do you think I'm doing?'

'Ha ha,' says Tilda, stabbing a gobbet of sausage with her plastic fork. 'You know what I mean.'

'No, Tilds, I really don't.'

'Talking to that Harry bloke . . . the prefect guy.'

'So I'm not allowed to talk to anyone now?'

'Don't act all innocent. I saw the way you smiled at him.'

'I don't know what you're talking about.'

'Yes you do.'

59

Her little red face is starting to do my head in. 'I don't actually, Tilda. But I'm sure you're going to tell me.'

'You were flirting with him.'

'What? No, you're joking aren't you?' My laugh comes out a bit fake.

'You were all over the guy.'

'We were just talking . . . about *Pygmalion*.'

'Yeah, right.'

'We were actually.'

'You can't do this, okay?'

'Do what?'

'Get close to anyone. Well, not another boy anyway. We talked about this. Don't you remember?'

'Trust me, Tilda, me and Harry are never going to "get close".'

'So it's Harry now, is it?'

(I suppose that's how I'll have to think of him from now on.)'That's his name. What else do you want me to call him?' I know she's scared, but I just wish she could see it my way. 'Oh come on, Tilds, it's not —'

'*Please*, just don't be an idiot, okay? You know what happened last time. If you carry on like this, it'll be the same story all over again.'

OCTOBER

Is there anything more pitiful than the child who courts popularity, mistakenly believing that membership of the 'right' peer group will somehow enhance their underdeveloped sense of identity? And what could be more irksome than the teacher who believes a rudimentary knowledge of popular culture will endear himself to his pupils?

Dido's Lament: 1,000 Things I Hate about School

14

FASHION

Tilda was wrong. I've been at St Thomas's nearly a month now, and as far as I can tell it's all going fine. I've drip-fed enough boring 'facts' about myself to keep the online stalkers off my back; according to Miss Hoolyhan, I'm exceeding my targets in everything except German; and the rest of my tutor group seem perfectly happy for me to listen in on their conversations and even offer the occasional opinion about gay marriage or push-up bras.

As for Harry, I've more or less managed to avoid him. In fact, if I didn't know any better, I'd say he was trying to avoid me too; except that when we do meet, in English or down in the learning resources centre, he's actually pretty friendly. So I guess it's all worked out for the best.

Things are better at home too. Tilda seems to have calmed down at last, Dad's doing impressions of 1980s comedians I've never even heard of again, and Mum doesn't look like a bomb's about to go off. I ought to be really happy. So what's the matter with me?

Maybe 'fitting in' isn't enough any more; maybe I want to be part of something. But it's virtually impossible with Katherine trailing me round the school like an over-opinionated spaniel. That's not fair. I've read her blog and it's actually pretty funny and I love the way she doesn't seem to give a shit. I just wish she was a bit less conscientious about the whole mentoring thing. And I'm sitting on the steps outside the art block, half listening to Katherine's theory about girls who spend entire decades obsessing over 'abstruse details of their wedding receptions' being more likely to gas themselves, when Magda and Izzy float tantalisingly into view. I've finally worked out how to tell them apart. They're like those TV presenters – Magda always stands on the right.

'Hi, Lauren,' Magda says, somehow managing to simultaneously smile at me and give Katherine the cold shoulder. 'Have you got a minute?'

'Yeah, sure, what is it?'

Izzy sucks on an imaginary lemon. 'In private, yeah? There's something we want to talk to you about.'

'Why can't she talk here?' says Katherine.

'It won't take long,' says Magda. 'But it's really important.'

'Found a cure for cancer, have we?' says Katherine.

'Not exactly, but when we find a cure for the ugly gene, we'll let you know.'

'Yeah, funny,' says Katherine.

'I'll just see what they want, shall I?' I say, trying to sound like I'm not that bothered.

Katherine looks even more disgusted with life than usual. 'You're not serious, are you, Lauren? Do you honestly want to talk to the Barbie twins?'

'Two seconds, okay?'

I follow them across to the rubbish bins at the back of the canteen. Izzy turns excitedly. 'Can I tell her now?'

Magda nods, her hair bouncing healthily, like a conditioner advert. 'Yeah, go for it.'

Izzy takes a step towards me. Instinctively, I back away. 'Don't look so nervous, Lauren. It's good news, I promise.'

'Oh . . . right, what is it?'

'You're into fashion, aren't you?'

Another flash of panic. 'How do you know that?'

'I saw what you said on Facebook about colour blocking,' says Magda.

'And that skater dress you're making in textiles is amazing,' says Izzy.

I'm dead chuffed by that. 'Do you think so?'

'Yeah, definitely. That's why we want to make sure you're coming to the meeting.'

'What meeting?'

'About the fashion show we're organising. Didn't you see the notice?'

'Er, no . . . sorry.'

'It's for Movember,' says Magda.

'What's Movember?'

'You must have seen it on telly. It's where celebrities

65

grow moustaches to raise awareness of male cancers and depression and stuff.'

'We were going to do a fashion show last year,' says Izzy. 'But there was all that fuss about the drama teacher and the girl "who cannot be named for legal reasons . . ."' (She breaks off and looks at Magda – 'Hannah Taylor!' they chorus together.) 'Anyway, I reckon this year they think it'll be good publicity.'

'And Catchpole's dad died of one of them,' says Magda. 'Cancer not depression, I think – so he was well up for it. He said we can choose any theme we like as long as Miss Hoolyhan supervises everything and we incorporate the school values.'

'Sounds great,' I say. 'But what do you want *me* to do?'

'We thought you could help out with some of the planning,' says Izzy. 'It'd be great to have someone who knows what they're talking about.'

'Really?'

'Totally,' says Magda. 'There's a meeting after school tomorrow in the art room. You will come, won't you, Lauren?'

Katherine's still going mental when we walk into English. 'A fashion show? A *fashion* show! That's just about typical of this school, isn't it? We can't even do Shakespeare without turning it into a tabloid fantasy. You're not seriously thinking about going, are you?'

'Yeah, kind of, why shouldn't I?'

'How long have you got?'

'It sounds . . . interesting. And it is for charity.'

'Oh yes,' says Katherine, swatting imaginary Magdas and Izzys with her copy of *Pygmalion*. 'The little sisters of mercy are saints in the making.'

'I thought it might be a good way of getting to know people.'

'What do you want to do that for?'

Ever tried explaining the rules of badminton to a horse? 'Well, you see . . .' But I've got a better idea. I know she acts all tough, but underneath, I have a feeling she might be kind of lonely. 'Actually I was going to ask you to come along with me, Katherine.'

'You are joking, of course.'

'No, it would be . . . nice to have you there.'

Katherine turns a slightly darker shade of pale. 'Really? Well, I am supposed to be looking out for you.'

'What, *still*?'

'Hoolyhan said I should keep an eye on you until the end of term. And come to think of it, what *is* so special about you, anyway?'

'Nothing . . . just —'

'I mean, no offence, Lauren, but you're actually kind of ordinary. Are you sure you're not ill or something?'

'Do I look ill?'

'Not really, no. So why does Hoolyhan think you need a minder?'

'Well, I suppose —'

Harry has been carefully laying out his ballpoint pens. 'Did someone mention the fashion show?'

That's surely not a hint of red on Katherine's cheeks? 'Yes. For some unknown reason, Lauren here wants to be part of the ridiculous fiasco.'

'Then we'll probably be seeing a lot more of each other,' says Harry, gathering up his ballpoints and starting all over again.

'What do you mean?' I say.

'Magda and Izzy have asked me to be the compere.'

15

ST THOMAS'S REUNITED

Katherine approaches the art block like a vegetarian on a school outing to the abattoir.

I try to disguise my nerves by asking her stupid questions. 'Why do you think Miss Hoolyhan always wears black?'

'She's in mourning for her life,' says Katherine. 'Well, wouldn't you be?'

'And what's with the history teacher who thinks it's still 1994?'

'Right, this is it,' says Katherine. 'Abandon hope all ye who enter here.'

The art room is full of half-finished GCSE art projects: a papier-mâché severed head with brightly coloured vomit dripping from its mouth, assorted charcoal drawings of dead rock stars, Cristiano Ronaldo in a ballet dress, and a whole host of nightmares in progress.

That hasn't stopped half the female population of St Thomas's turning up. It's standing room only, and the excitement is so tangible you could probably cut it with some dressmaking shears. Best of all, Tilda's here too – right at the back next to the store cupboard. Maybe we could work on some ideas together; it would be just like old times. I call out my sister's name, but she doesn't hear me. And the next thing I know she's disappeared into a babbling flash mob of Year Ten girls.

The boys are a bit thin on the ground though. Miss Hoolyhan is chatting to a little bearded guy in a Kraftwerk T-shirt, a couple of brave Year Sevens are huddled together under Kurt Cobain, and there's Harry, making sure the paintbrushes are the 'right' way up. He nods and smiles at me. I nod and smile back, surprised at the warm scary feeling in my stomach.

Magda and Izzy are standing in formation at the front. They don't look best pleased when they see who my 'plus one' is.

'What did you have to bring her for?' says Izzy.

'Hello, Isobel,' says Katherine, in her best poshed-up Liza Doolittle. 'How . . . do . . . you . . . do?'

'You know what this meeting's about, don't you?' says Magda. 'It's about a fashion show not a . . . a . . . a Geography assessment.'

Miss Hoolyhan's smile is ninety per cent sweetness, ten per cent bite. 'I thought the whole point was that anyone in the school could get involved. After all, tolerance is one of our core values.'

Izzy eyes Katherine suspiciously. 'Are you absolutely sure you want to be here?'

'Oh absolutely,' says Katherine, provocatively fluttering her mascara-free eyelashes. 'All I ever wanted was to be a supermodel. *It's my dream.*'

'Can we get on please, Magda?' says Miss Hoolyhan. 'I've got a mountain of marking waiting for me.'

'Okay, right, yeah, let's . . .' Magda takes a sip of Evian and flashes her teeth. 'So, first off we want to thank you all for coming. As you all know, Izzy and I have been planning a charity fashion show. We're very excited about it, and we hope you will be too.'

Izzy takes over. 'We think it's a great way of bringing the whole school together – as well as raising money for a fantastic cause. We've even designed our own logo.' She holds up a laminated poster with a Photoshopped picture of various different types of clothing holding hands.

And just in case we can't read, they chant the slogan together: '*St Thomas's Community College. A school united by clothes.*'

The bearded guy next to Miss Hoolyhan lets out an audible snigger.

'Our theme will be the four seasons,' says Magda. 'I'll be producing – and modelling, of course – and Izzy's going to be our resident stylist. But we'll need lots of help – that's where you guys come in.'

The girl with the violin case has her hand up. 'What sort of look will you be going for?'

'Good question, Clare,' says Magda. 'I'm interested in the old classics with a touch of subversive glamour. A

71

well-cut trench coat is as relevant now as it's ever been, and soft florals can look amazing with chunky boots.'

Katherine rolls her eyes at me.

'We've already approached the local stores and boutiques,' says Izzy. 'And they're very happy for us to model some of their designs. We'll have to accessorise, of course. But prom dresses are always a money spinner.'

'You should get that girl in Year Eight to model maternity outfits.'

'Yes, thank you, Candice-Marie,' says Miss Hoolyhan. 'That's not really appropriate, is it?'

'No, miss.'

'How many models do you need?' says the violin girl.

'We'll have to find a few more boys, of course,' says Magda. 'But round about twenty girls for sixty outfits.'

An audible groan rumbles around the art room.

'There'll be plenty of other jobs too,' says Izzy. 'We need loads of dressers and someone to sort out the tickets and design a website. Harry Heasman's going to be our compere and George has very kindly come back from sixth-form college to help out with the light show.'

'All right, Grunt?' calls a voice from the back.

The little bearded bloke waves and mumbles 'hi'.

'Okay,' says Magda. 'Any more questions?'

'Have you thought about the music yet?' says Miss Hoolyhan. 'Because I'm sure the wind band could manage "Summer Nights" from *Grease*.'

'*No*,' says Magda. 'It's probably easier if we stick to

recorded music, thanks, miss. And anyway we're going to ask a few members of staff to be models. And we'd like you to be one of them.'

'Really?' says Miss Hoolyhan. 'How exciting.'

I hadn't intended to put my hand up, but I just can't help myself. I've been planning imaginary fashions shows since I was thirteen. 'Why don't we have a big screen at the top of the catwalk and project photos on to it? Paris in the spring, stuff like that. We could synchronise it all with the music.'

'I see where you're coming from,' says Izzy. 'But I'm not sure we'll have time.'

'I'll do it if you like,' I say, already trying to remember the name of that French photographer. 'I could operate the whole thing from my laptop.'

'I think it's a great idea,' says Harry. 'What do you think, Mags?'

Magda plays with her hair. 'Well, if you think you can do it, Lauren, that would be amazing.'

'Fine, I'll get on to it as soon as you decide on the music.'

'Great,' says Magda. 'But you won't be able to operate it on the night, because you'll be far too busy modelling.'

'Will I?' (If I wrote my own dreams, they'd probably open with a scene like this.)

'That's right,' says Izzy. 'We've got some denim shorts to die for. And there's a yellow beach dress that would look perfect on you.'

73

But then it hits me. What if someone's taking photographs? What if there's a picture in the local paper or something? And it'll be a nightmare backstage. Suddenly it doesn't seem like such a brilliant idea. 'I'm really sorry, Magda, but I don't think I'll be able to do the modelling.'

'But you've got to,' says Magda.

'We need you,' says Izzy. 'You've got the height for it, and your legs are amazing.'

'Look, I'm sorry, I can't,' I say, not quite so panicky that I don't enjoy the compliments. 'I'll be operating the laptop, won't I?'

'No way,' says Magda. 'Your little friend here —' she flares her nostrils at Katherine — 'can push a few buttons. And I'm sure George could use some help with the lights.'

'I think Katherine wants to be a model,' I say.

Katherine wipes away an imaginary tear. 'It's hard to see my dreams trampled on like that, but if it's what Magda wants I'll do my best to work that pesky computer and help George with the lights.'

'Well, there you go, Lauren,' says Izzy. 'All sorted.'

'Look, I don't know. I'll have to think about it.'

'You'd better make your mind up soon,' says Magda. 'We're starting rehearsals next week.'

'Lauren . . . Lauren . . . hang on a minute. Can we talk for a second?'

'What is it?'

Miss Hoolyhan has followed me out to the courtyard. She rests a black-cardiganed elbow on the recycling bin and tries to catch her breath. 'Are you . . . are you nervous about it?'

'About what?'

'Modelling in the fashion show. I know I am.'

'What have I got to be nervous about?'

'Nothing . . . nothing,' says Miss Hoolyhan, smoothing the front of her black knee-length skirt. 'It's just that Katherine told me about your panic attack in PE.'

'Oh . . . right.'

'And I know you get a bit claustrophobic. So I just wondered if you were slightly anxious about changing with the others.'

'No, of course not, I . . .' But what's the point in trying to hide it? I take a deep breath. 'Look, I know it sounds silly, but it's the kind of situation I try to avoid.'

'I thought so,' said Miss Hoolyhan. 'I tell you what; I'm going to be changing in the equipment store at the back of the sports hall. I'd have to okay it with Mr Catchpole, but I'm sure you could share with me if it makes you feel more comfortable. And if anyone asks, just tell them I need some help with that ball gown.'

'Thanks, miss. That would certainly make things easier. But I'm still not sure I can do it.'

'You want to, though, don't you, Lauren?'

'Well, yes, but —'

'Have a word with your mum. I could never talk to

my mother,' she adds gloomily, 'but you seem to have a very healthy relationship with yours.'

If she's really in mourning for her life, I think it's sad. Miss Hoolyhan's probably the nicest teacher I've ever met.

16

MR REASONABLE

'And you think it's a good idea, do you?' says Mum, decapitating a king prawn and dumping its severed head in the bin.

'I'm not sure. What do you think?'

It's like one of those public consultations that Dad's always moaning about where they ask if you want them to close down the post office or build a new runway in your back garden, but they've made up their minds already. 'Maybe it's something you should avoid for a while. It's a big step, Lauren.'

'Not really, Mum. It's only a small school thing. And I love fashion – you know that.'

'Yes, of course,' says Mum, drowning courgettes in olive oil. 'But I have a feeling your father will be none too thrilled about it.'

'So don't tell him.'

'We don't do secrets any more, Lauren,' says Mum

pointedly. 'But before I talk to him, I need you to be certain about this.'

'I am certain. At least, I think I am.'

'I'm not saying don't do it, exactly. I just don't want to see you running before you can walk.'

And I can almost see her mind ticking over as she tries to lighten the moment with a lame joke.

'Huh . . . Catwalk!'

I thought Big Moe would be on my side, but two minutes into the call and he's doing his 'Mr Reasonable' act. 'You can't really blame your ma, you know. She's only trying to look out for you.'

'I don't blame her. I just wish she'd try a bit harder to understand.'

'Are you kidding? If it wasn't for Nikki you wouldn't even be —'

'Yeah, yeah, I know, but —'

Somewhere down the corridor a riot is brewing. 'Keep it down, people. I'm trying to have a conversation here.' I'd forgotten how scary Big Moe can be when he raises his voice. 'Sorry . . . Lauren, what were you saying?'

'It feels like she's never going to let me go. All I want is my life back.'

Moe laughs. 'Now how many times have I heard that one before?'

I swear the damp patch under my bedroom window is getting bigger, like an oversized human head is trying to force its way through the wall. If I moved the bed I could hide it, I suppose, but it would still be there, so what's the point?

'Tell me what *you* think, Moe. What should I do?'

'It's not about what I think.'

'Yeah, but if you were me, you'd go for it, right?'

And I don't need to be in the same room as him to know that he's stroking his beard and probably planning his next 'brew'. 'Well, you remember that little saying of mine, don't you?'

Big Moe had lots of little sayings. 'Er . . .'

'It doesn't matter what the experts say, the only person who really knows what you're going through is you.'

'So you're saying I should do it then?'

'I'm not saying anything.'

'Yes, but —'

There's a loud crash in the background. 'Got to go, Lauren. Speak to you soon.'

There's an even louder crash in the foreground as Tilda bursts into my bedroom. 'I can't believe you!'

'Hi, Tilds, what's up?'

'Are you for real?'

'What are you talking about?'

'The fashion show. You're not seriously thinking of modelling, are you?'

'I am, as it happens. And anyway, you were at the meeting, I thought you wanted to do it too.'

'No way. Not if you are. I walked out the moment that

Izzy girl mentioned denim shorts. I knew you wouldn't be able to resist it.'

'Oh come on, Tilds. It could be a laugh if we do it together.'

'You're joking, aren't you?'

'Remember when we recreated London Fashion Week in your bedroom?'

'Yeah, but that was before —'

'Nothing's going to happen, Tilda. Please, just give me a break for once.'

'I can't believe you're even considering it. You seriously want to get up on stage with half the school staring at you? And you can bet your life at least one of them will be filming it on their bloody phone, so it's bound to turn up on YouTube. Is that what you want?'

'I'm not hiding for the rest of my life.'

'Everything was going fine. Why do you have to be like this?'

'Look, I've made up my mind, so just leave it, yeah?'

'Typical. Do what the hell you like and sod the rest of us.'

'I'm your sister, Tilda. Doesn't that count for anything?'

'You're not my sister, okay?'

17

WALK LIKE A WOMAN

They've marked out a catwalk in white tape on the sports hall floor. Izzy and Magda insist on calling it 'the runway' – the correct term for a classier, more intimate type of show.

We take it in turns to practise walking towards them, trying to keep pace with the thumping techno beat. Katherine and the boy from the sixth-form college who everyone calls 'Grunt' are exchanging sly witticisms over the CD player, experimenting with sound levels and smirking like satirical gnomes.

Magda and Izzy have obviously opted for the good cop bad cop approach:

'No, no, no,' screams Magda. 'You mustn't forget the stops. Bend your front leg, put your hand on your hip and pose. How hard can it be?'

A trio of Year Seven girls are millimetres from tears.

'Look, I know it's difficult in school uniform,' says Izzy. 'But try and be a bit more . . . you know, girlie.'

Katherine and the boy in the *Give Quiche a Chance* T-shirt snort in perfect harmony.

'Right, let's have the next lot please,' says Magda. 'And try to put some feeling into it.'

A couple of girls and the goalkeeper who can't kick straight manage to make it to the end of the runway without totally embarrassing themselves, but the only 'shoot' the rest of them are fit for is the type that involves a firing squad. And the teachers are even worse: Mr Catchpole takes dad-dancing to a whole new level, Miss Hoolyhan should be walking behind the coffin at a Victorian funeral and Mr Peel, the time-warped history teacher, looks like an ageing rock star with piles.

So when it comes to my turn, I'm actually quite confident about it, even when I realise who my partner is.

'All right, Dizzy?' says Conor Corcoran, who for some reason fancies himself as the next face of Versace. 'Don't worry, babe, I'm right behind you – nice arse, by the way.'

As soon as I start walking, I forget him completely, gliding down the runway as smoothly as I'd always imagined. I may not be Kate Moss exactly, but I've been practising this in my head since the Year Six leavers' barbecue, and now that I'm up here at last, I have to admit, it's even better than I thought. For once in my life, I'm in the right place at the right time.

'Thank God someone knows what they're doing,' says Izzy. 'You're a natural, Lauren. You sure you've never done this sort of thing before?'

'Only in my sister's bedroom.'

'Okay, stop the music,' says Magda. 'I said stop the music. You two on the sound system, quit messing about.'

The music eventually splutters and dies.

'Now as you can see,' says Magda, 'we have a lot of work to do.'

'Sorry about the stops, guys,' says Mr Peel. 'I'll be better when I get some decent music.'

Magda isn't quite so optimistic. 'Some of you girls have absolutely no idea. And you're not even in heels yet.'

'Why don't you show them, Lauren?' says Izzy.

'Show them what?'

'How to walk properly. They look more like a herd of cage fighters at the moment.'

Magda claps her hands. 'All right, you lot, shut up and listen to Lauren.'

I step out in front of them, hiding my anxiety behind a semi-hysterical smile. But at least I know what I'm talking about. 'Right, the first thing you've got to do is take smaller steps, yeah? And turn your elbows in towards the waist, so your palms face the front. Okay, guys, can we have some music please?'

This time the sound system works perfectly.

'Right, let's just walk around the sports hall together. There's no need to be self-conscious, no one's judging you. And always remember, you're doing this for yourself, not to look good for some guy.'

The Year Sevens are really getting into it.

'That's great, much better. Now smile, and lift your chins. It's such a boy thing to stare at your feet. And take in the sights as you go, don't focus on your final destination.'

Miss Hoolyhan looks almost carefree for once, sweeping round the sports hall in her long black skirt, her head held high.

'Now, last but not least, swing your hips – *but make it subtle.*'

I'm not pretending they've suddenly turned into super-models, but at least they don't look scared any more.

And Magda looks happier too. 'Yeah, not bad,' she admits grudgingly.

'By George, I think they've got it,' says Katherine, exchanging a nerdy high-five (minimal hand contact, shoulder level at best) with her bearded associate.

But she can take the piss as much as she likes for all I care, because right now I'm feeling pretty good about myself. No one's laughing at me. No one's trying to kill me. They're actually listening to me and even doing what I say. It's almost like I've found my voice at last.

Mr Catchpole is loading babies (the type they hand out in Year Ten to stop you getting pregnant) into the back of his yellow Corsa SXi. I try to glide past him, but he stumbles across the grass verge towards me, modelling a late-twentieth-century Marks & Spencer jacket.

'That was . . . fascinating, Lauren. I think you could teach us all a thing or two.'

'Thank you, sir.'

'I'm glad I've caught you.'

'Are you?'

'Yes,' he says, baby in one hand, Tesco bag in the other. 'I thought you might like to know that I've made contact with your last school.'

A hand grenade explodes in my stomach. 'Why would you do that?'

'They called me actually.'

'What for? Who was it?'

'I can't recall the name, I'm afraid. But it was someone from the senior management team.'

'And you're quite sure it was really a teacher?'

'Yes, of course. Look, I'm sure there's nothing sinister about this, Lauren. They just wanted to know how you were settling in.'

'And what did you tell them?'

'I told them you were doing fine.' A troubling thought crumples his overripe features. 'You are doing fine, aren't you, Lauren?'

I was until about twenty seconds ago. 'Yes, yes I think so.'

A baby is wailing in the boot of his car. He turns towards it like an anxious parent. 'I'd better . . . Goodnight, Lauren. Look, I'm sorry if I upset you just now. I thought you'd be pleased to know that someone from your old stomping ground was still thinking about you. There's really nothing to worry about.'

But I'm still a bit shaky as I pass through the school gates and head down the hill, which is probably why I overreact when a perfectly manicured finger taps me on the shoulder.

'*Oh my God!*'

'What's the matter?' says Izzy. 'Calm down, Lauren, it's only me.'

'Oh . . . right . . . it's you. Sorry, you made me jump.' Why's she on her own? That's a bit scary in itself. 'Where's Magda?'

'We're not joined at the hip, you know.' It's the first time I've heard Izzy raise her voice. A millisecond later, the familiar smile is back in place. 'She had to pick up her little brother from football.'

Izzy really does have the most beautiful highlights. I half wonder about asking where she gets them done. 'Oh, right.'

'You were great back there by the way. Thanks for helping out. Poor Mags was getting really frazzled.'

'Yeah, I noticed.'

'She just wants it to be perfect. We both do.'

'Yeah, course.'

'Listen, Lauren, what are you doing on Saturday night?'

The same as usual: watching *Casualty* and putting up with my dad's crap jokes. Of course I don't tell Izzy that. 'Oh, you know, busy busy busy.'

'Well, there's a "gathering" at my place if you're interested.'

'Er, yes, I —'

'And your mum will let you come?'

'Eh?'

'She sounds a bit full on, that's all.'

'Oh no, she's not that bad really.' A half-truth slips out. 'My . . . *sister* had some trouble with bullying, so she tends to be a bit overprotective.'

'She should tell old Catchpole. It's his favourite subject – and STDs, of course.'

'Yeah, I noticed.'

'So you'll try and make it then?'

'Yeah, thanks. It's not your birthday, is it?'

'No, it's my parents' wedding anniversary.'

'Oh, right.'

'So they're in Florence for the weekend. You can stay over if you like.'

'I doubt I'd be able to —'

'But don't bring that awful girl with the pigtail. Magda can't stand the sight of her. I have no idea why you let her follow you around all day.'

'Well, she —'

'Just you, all right?'

I'm pretty sure the feeling's mutual, so I'm probably doing Katherine a favour here. 'Okay, fine. But I don't even know where you live.'

Izzy waves at the blue Citroën C4 Picasso that's pulled up on the other side of the road. The door opens and she walks towards it. 'I'll Facebook you.'

18

IT'S MY PARTY
(AND I'LL PUKE IF I WANT TO)

Have you ever met someone with trichotillomania? Well, if you haven't, Tilda's doing a pretty good impersonation of one right now. She's pretending to watch *Queer Eye for the Straight Guy* on her laptop, but as far as I can see she's far more interested in trying to pull her hair out.

'You look nice, Lauren,' says Mum, surreptitiously running her eye over my ensemble. 'Are you sure you're going to be warm enough?'

'Yes, Mum, I'll be fine.'

I've had too many 'You're not going out like that, are you?' conversations with Dad to risk the strapless dress we bought in the States. That's why I've opted for a knee-length red skirt, white scoop-neck top and my old bomber jacket. No heels either – or someone's bound to go on about how tall I am and I hate that – just my favourite blue Converse All-Stars. I'm keeping my hair up too. No point confusing everyone with a total makeover, but I think I'll still pass.

'Will there be any . . . alcohol there?' says Mum, reaching for her pre-*Casualty* glass of red.

Tilda lets go of her hair for a moment. 'What do *you* think?'

'So what if there is?' I say. 'I don't drink anyway, you know that.'

I've promised Mum I'm never going to hurt her again. Sometimes I have a feeling she doesn't believe me. 'Oh, it's not you that I'm worried about, Lauren. It's the others. Did you know that British teenagers caused over a hundred and thirty-four million pounds' worth of damage at parties last year?'

I can't help laughing.

Mum smiles too. 'It's not funny you know. She hasn't put anything about the party on Facebook, has she?'

'Izzy's not stupid, Mum. You'd like her, she's really nice.'

Dad appears, grim-faced in the doorway, the spitting image of the guys who escort dead bodies to funerals. 'You're sure about this, are you?'

Tilda looks up from her screen.

Mum takes another sip/gulp. 'She's sure, aren't you, Lauren? Now off you go and have a great time.'

You know what really annoys me about my dad? The fact he genuinely believes his new Corolla is a 'cool car'. I can almost hear his inner monologue as we turn into the main road and start accelerating: *Eight airbags as standard, stain-resistant heated front seats, premium audio with navigation and a dedicated APP suite, not to mention automatic climate control – just slip her into cruise mode and away we go.*

But then, unfortunately, he starts to speak. 'I see United are in for that Danish bloke.'

'Are they, Dad?'

'Doesn't mean they'll get him though.'

'No, Dad.'

He flicks on his favourite 'old guy' radio station. 'You must know this one. I used to love the Sex Pistols. Nearly saw them live once.'

Please don't sing, Dad. Please don't sing.

And perhaps there is a God because instead of screaming along with it he turns the volume down. 'I've had a letter from your grandma.'

My belief in God wavers again. 'Oh, right.'

'She wants to see you. I thought we could drive down at half-term.'

'I don't get it. I thought she never wanted to see me again.'

Dad clears his throat. 'That's not really what she said.'

'So what's her bloody problem then?'

Even the Sex Pistols can't quite cover the awkward silence. Dad reaches for a travel sweet. 'I think you know what her problem is.'

'Yeah, and that's why I'm not going.'

'Please, Lauren. She's obviously desperate to see you. And, well, it . . . it might be your last chance.'

'Grandma's not dying, is she?'

'No, no, of course not. But when you get to eighty-four, you don't know how long you've got.'

I've not seen Grandma in over two years. And I miss her. 'What does she want, anyway?'

'She says she's got something for you. But I think she just wants to see how you are.'

Every summer, Tilda and I spent a week at the house in Littlehampton. I loved Grandma more than almost anything. Mum and Dad were always in a hurry. But Grandma always seemed to have time. If you couldn't sleep, she'd never pack you off to bed and order you to 'think great thoughts', she'd fix you sugary tea with a ginger biscuit and tell you the story of Auntie Mabel's knitting and the toffee apple.

'All right, if she really wants to see me, I'll go. But if the old dear starts having another go at me, I'm out of there, okay?'

'Fine,' says Dad. 'I'll phone and let her know we're coming.'

The sat nav politely informs us we've arrived at our destination. Dad pulls up in front of an oak-beamed mansion (well, compared to our crappy new house it's a mansion) with a double garage and a classic MGB road-ster in the drive. Now *that* is a cool car.

'Here we are then,' says Dad, undoing his seat belt. 'Do you want me to come to the door with you?'

'You are joking, aren't you?'

'Of course I am,' says Dad, re-fastening his seat belt. 'Now remember, I'll be waiting out here for you at eleven. So don't be late.'

'That's way too early.'

'It's what we agreed on. If you're not out by five past, I'm coming to get you.'

'Okay, fine,' I say, jumping out onto the pavement before he can come up with any more ridiculous conditions. 'I'll see you later.'

The passenger window slides down; Dad shouts some last-minute instructions. 'Watch what you're drinking, don't say anything you might regret later, and make sure your phone's switched on.'

'Yes, Dad.'

'And, Lauren?'

'Yes.'

'You look . . . nice.'

The house is throbbing at 120 bpm. I turn to face the music, acutely aware that Dad's still monitoring my every move from the car. When I reach the front door, I start waving at him. And I keep waving until he finally takes the hint and drives off.

It's probably for the best, because just as I'm about to knock, my breathing goes all funny and I bottle it.

I walk the streets for nearly an hour – only as far as the postbox and back, but over and over until the cracks in the pavement start to feel like old friends. That's nothing

– there were a couple of times last year when I slipped out of the house at two in the morning and didn't sneak back until sunrise. I still feel safest when there's no one about.

You see, you think you're ready for something, but it's never quite that simple. Izzy's party ought to be the best moment of my new life so far. But what if one of them gets totally shitfaced and starts asking dumb questions? Three times I nearly give in and call Dad. He'd love that, wouldn't he? But it's not the inspirational 'notes to self' in my head that send me scuttling back to Izzy's house, it's the weather. Thank God I didn't wear that strapless dress. Somewhere on the way to the postbox, autumn turned into winter, and it's so bloody cold that I'm shivering like a five-year-old on Littlehampton beach.

This time the front door is wide open. The violin girl from the fashion show welcomes me with a big hug. 'Hi, Lauren. You look gorgeous.'

'Thanks.'

'There's, like, pizza in the kitchen and dancing down that way, I think. Or you could try your luck upstairs!'

And suddenly I feel really self-conscious: small and insignificant and completely out of place. Maybe if I track down the person who invited me, I might feel like I belong here. 'Where's Izzy, by the way?'

'Dunno. Last time I saw her she was with that Rod guy.'

'Right, I'll go have a look.'

I follow the music to a darkened room where a First

World War scenario is playing out. The boys are lined up down one side with their Peronis and Kronenbourgs and the girls are camped opposite, texting and previewing the occasional dance move. Maybe by Christmas – or sooner if someone puts the right song on – some of them might get it together in no man's land.

They all look at least five years older without their school uniforms. I barely recognise anyone. But they seem to know me. Both sides of the conflict shout friendly greetings and wave their phones/beer bottles at me. I wave back, scanning the hormone-scented shadows for Izzy. But there's no sign of her, so I decide to try somewhere else.

Down in the kitchen, there's a competition to see who can stuff their face with the most grapes. And the conservatory is playing host to a face-sucking tournament. Mouths wide open, eyes tight shut, the only clues to the players' identities are the backs of their heads. The ombré-style curls almost certainly belong to Magda, but there's not a single highlight to be seen.

So I creep upstairs, still shivering even though I'm not cold any more, past the paintings of horses and ballet dancers and a photo of a cute little Izzy with an owl on her shoulder.

Knocking softly on the first random door, I turn the handle and push it open.

A ten-year-old assassin, who's far too young for China Lake grenade launchers, is communing with his Xbox. 'Oi, piss off!' he screams, which is exactly what I do, as a barrage of Lego and Hula Hoops drives me back into the hallway and through the door opposite.

They may call it the smallest room in the house, but this one is bigger than my bedroom. Down at the far end, some beautiful highlights are slowly disappearing down the toilet. I guess that's my hostess.

'Hi – Izzy, are you okay?'

Somewhere between puking and sobbing she manages to get most of a sentence out. 'I'm fine. Just leave me alone — *plurgghh . . .*'

'Yeah, sure.'

I exit the bathroom. But I can't go downstairs again. Not yet anyway. I need a few minutes on my own to regroup. This time I'm more careful, listening at the next bedroom first, before venturing in. And it looks promising: soft lighting and a huge double bed with a pile of coats on it. But my heart plummets like a learner swimmer in the deep end when I see who's stretched out alongside them.

'All right, Dizzy? What's up?'

'I'm looking for someone.'

The straw trilby is exactly what I'd expect from Conor Corcoran. But what's he doing with a biro in his hand? 'Well, it must be your lucky day then, because now you've found me.'

'No, no, I didn't mean —'

'Is it hot in here, or is it just you?'

'Yeah, it is quite war— Oh . . . right.'

Conor Corcoran brushes aside a trio of Parkas and pats the bed. 'Why don't you come and sit down?'

'No thanks, I . . . What are you doing anyway?'

'Oh yeah, I found this. It's a right laugh.'

He appears to be scribbling in some kind of scrapbook. I edge nearer to see what he's up to. 'Is that what I think it is?'

'Yeah, brilliant, isn't it?'

It looks like a picture of Izzy in a lacy white dress. On closer inspection I realise it's her mum and dad's wedding photos. Conor has given the bride a beard and glasses and is about to start work on the groom. 'You can't do that, Conor! Stop it.'

'Oh come on, it's only a bit of fun.'

I grab his biro. 'You shouldn't mess about with photos. Photos are important. They're all that people have to remember stuff by.'

'What about the wedding video?'

'You can't just walk into someone's house and start defacing their property.'

'Oh come on, Dizzy, I was enjoying that. Give us my pen back.'

'Don't be an idiot.'

He jumps off the bed and steps towards me. 'All right then, if you're really that bothered about it, how about we get a bit more creative?'

'What are you talking about?'

'Can't you guess?'

96

'No.'

'Here's a clue then. If you were a burger I'd call you McBeautiful.'

'What?'

'Leave it out, Dizzy. You must know I like you.'

'Well, I'm sorry about that because —'

'It's okay, we can just talk if you like. Why don't you tell me about your old school?'

'*No*, I . . . it's too boring anyway. You don't want to hear about that.'

'I'm sure there's something else we could do,' he says with a massive metaphorical wink. 'You never know, you might enjoy it.'

And I'm looking around for a football to curb Conor's enthusiasm when in walks the deputy head student with a crash helmet under his arm.

19

A LITTLE TOUCH OF HARRY
IN THE NIGHT

'Talk about bad timing,' says Conor Corcoran. 'Bloody hell, Hazzer, don't you ever knock?'

'I need somewhere to put my helmet,' says Harry.

'Well, chuck it on the bed and do one, eh, matey? Me and Lauren want some quality one-on-one time.'

'Is that right?' says Harry, rearranging the coats into a straight line.

'Yes,' says Conor, grabbing my hand. 'We're an item, aren't we, babe?'

'Don't be stupid,' I say. 'And can I have my hand back, please?'

'I think you'd better let her go, Conor,' says Harry.

'Oh come on, Hazzer, give us a break.'

'I *said* I think you'd better let her go.'

'Yeah all right,' says Conor, releasing my hand and slumping back onto the bed. 'But I still reckon we could be good together.'

'Look, I'm sure you're a nice guy and everything, Conor, but I think I'm going downstairs.'

'That's what they all say.'

Back in the kitchen, they've abandoned grape-stuffing for chilli powder and Tabasco cocktails.

'You okay?' says Harry.

'Yeah, fine. It's just a bit hot in here.'

'Don't worry about Conor. He's an idiot sometimes, but I think he actually likes you.'

'Is that so hard to believe then?'

'That's not what I meant,' says Harry. 'I was trying to make you feel better.'

Skinny jeans really suit him, and so does that blue checked shirt. 'Yeah, I know . . . Thanks.'

'Can I get you a drink or something?'

There are so many questions I'm burning to ask him, so many things that I just can't say. 'I think I'd better call my dad.'

'You can't go yet,' says Harry. 'It's not even ten.'

'Well, I suppose I could stay for a bit.'

'Great,' says Harry. 'What do you want to do?'

And then I have an idea. 'The music's a bit crap, but we could go and have a dance if you like.'

'I don't dance,' says Harry.

'Really?' H used to be into some weird hard-core stuff. Maybe it's for the best.

'But I know what we can do.' He takes a paper

plate and piles it with pizza triangles. 'Pepperoni, right?'

'How did you —'

'Everyone likes pepperoni. And if you look under the sink, there's a plastic bag with some cans in it.'

'I don't drink.'

'Me neither, so you'd better bring that bottle of Diet Coke.'

'Where are we going?'

'Shh,' says Harry, pushing open the back door and stepping into the night. 'We're not supposed to be out here.'

'Why not?'

'Izzy's dad's a bit of a gardening freak. Breathe on his roses and you're dead.'

'How do you know that?'

'We went out for a bit. Me and Izzy, I mean, not me and her dad. That would be weird.'

'Right, yeah.'

There's enough light from the conservatory to guide us across the decking and out onto the lawn, past a trampoline shrouded in black netting and safely round the fish pond. But as soon as we slip through a gap in the hedge, the darkness takes hold.

There's a definite whiff of compost as Harry reaches for my hand. 'Watch out for rabbit holes. You don't want to twist your ankle or anything.'

'Where are we going?'

'You'll see,' says Harry.

And I'm trying to work out what it means, the hand-holding (does he really care about my ankles?), when we come to one of those fancy sheds with a proper slate roof and a veranda.

'What do you think?' says Harry.

'It's nice,' I say, half wondering if I've done the right thing.

'Hold this pizza a minute. I need to find something.'

'Are you sure we should be doing this, Harry? Won't somebody wonder where you are?'

'Don't worry,' he says, feeling under a flowerpot and pulling out a key. 'None of the others know about this place. Well, only Izzy. And I don't think she's up to hide-and-seek right now.'

'We don't want to get into trouble, do we?'

Harry laughs. Not the polite deputy head student chuckle designed to show Mrs Woolf he appreciates George Bernard Shaw's 'hilarious' phonetics gags, but more of a sarcastic *hmphh*, more like the H I once knew.

'What's so funny?'

'Nothing,' he says, fumbling for the light switch. 'It's just that I don't do trouble any more.'

'What do you mean?'

'I'm not that kind of person,' he says, dragging a couple of sun loungers to either side of a wooden picnic table and fiddling about with them until he gets the angles right. 'Bit boring really.'

'Maybe we should go back to the house.'

'We've only just got here. Sit down for a minute and I'll get things sorted.'

It's pretty posh for a garden shed: three times the size of my bedroom with an embroidered wall-hanging of a poppy field, fifty shades of electric gardening tools and even a fridge.

And I take back what I said about the crap music. That's my favourite Beatles song wafting down the garden. I relax back onto the musty-smelling lounger cushion and hum along with the chorus.

'How about a bit of atmosphere?' says Harry, laying out a symmetrical grotto of scented candles. 'Now where are those matches?' He roots around in a bucketful of golf putters and pulls out a box of Swan Vestas.

'Are you sure that's not a fire hazard?'

'Of course – I've done it loads of times,' says Harry, putting the flame to the one in the middle. 'And anyway, we should probably switch the light off – just in case.'

An unexpected pang of jealousy ambushes me in the candlelight. It's completely bonkers, of course, but I hate it that Harry and Izzy had a secret place too.

'This is good,' he says, taking a piece of pizza and stretching out alongside me. 'And about time too.'

'Eh?'

'We keep bumping into each other, don't we? But we've never had time for a proper chat.'

'No, I suppose not.'

'You always seem in such a hurry.'

It's true. Every time I see him in the corridor, I put my head down and keep walking. 'You know what it's like. I'm still settling in really.'

But what harm would it do? As far as he's concerned I'm a total stranger. Would it really be so terrible if we were 'just mates'?

I study his face in the flickering half-light. He looks back for a moment, before turning his attention to his feet.

We both speak at the same time:

'So what's it like being—'

'I was just wondering how —'

'No, you go first,' I say.

'I was just wondering how . . .' Halfway through the sentence he seems to change his mind. 'How you're getting on at school.'

'What are you, my dad or something?'

'Only asking.'

'I know, sorry, it's just that no one in my family can go ten seconds without asking me the same bloody question.'

'So what's that all about? Did you have a bad time at your last school?'

'Why? Should I have done?'

'I don't know. I just thought if your family are so paranoid, you might have had a few problems.'

'No, not really,' I say, grateful that he can't see my face changing colour. 'Let's just say they weren't exactly the happiest days of my life.'

'Yeah, I know what you mean.'

And now it's my turn to laugh. 'You're not seriously telling me you don't like school, are you, Harry? Mr Big Shot Prefect and everything. I've seen you standing at the front of the stage ordering kids about. You love it, you know you do.'

'Yeah, yeah, yeah,' he says, taking a slug of Diet Coke. 'Life is good. Well, most of the time.'

'And I bet it's nice to be popular.'

'You're actually quite popular yourself, Lauren.'

'Don't be silly.'

'I'm dead serious. Why do you think Magda wants you in her little extravaganza?'

And I'm almost starting to enjoy myself when Harry makes his move.

'You know if you pull the armrests, like this, it makes the whole seat go down.' My sun lounger tilts backwards like a dentist's chair and suddenly I'm flat on my back with Harry standing over me.

'Hey, you know what we should do?' he whispers.

There was definite chemistry between us before, but it was more the kind of chemistry that made explosions. This is different.

'No, what?' I say, half closing my eyes.

'We should play this game I invented,' says Harry, disappearing into the shadows for a moment and coming back with a huge sack of daffodil bulbs. 'See that watering can hanging on the wall? It's five points every time you get one in. First to fifty. Loser has to do a forfeit.'

As soon as we start throwing bulbs about, the conversation starts to flow. No difficult questions, just a list of our top ten favourite movies, a slight disagreement over possible music for the fashion show, a brief rundown of his football team's defensive problems and a debate about whether being able to eat as much pizza as you want and not put on weight is actually a superpower. Half an hour later, the floor is strewn with bulbs like the aftermath of a gardeners' orgy, both of us are breathing harder and I've thrashed him 50–10.

'In your face, "Hazzer".'

'So come on then, what's my forfeit?'

The first one that springs to mind is instantly quarantined. 'Don't know really. I —'

'You'd better think of something. This is a "for one night only" chance in a lifetime, Lauren.'

My top lip curls upwards into a sly smile. 'Okay, then. How about this? We're going to bounce on that trampoline while you sing me a song from *The Lion King*.'

'I don't think so,' says Harry.

'Why not?'

'It's cold out there. And someone might see us.'

'That's why they call it a forfeit, moron.'

'Okay, but we'd better tidy up first.'

'We can do that later.'

'No, I just —'

'Come on,' I say, grabbing his hand and leading him up the garden path. 'Not chicken, are you?'

'This is such a bad idea,' says Harry.

'It's a great idea. I love trampolines.'

'Yeah, but you haven't heard me sing.'

(That's what *he* thinks.) I pull aside the black netting and start climbing in.

'Take your shoes off first,' says Harry. 'Izzy's dad would go apeshit.'

'You're such a good boy, aren't you?'

'Am I?' says Harry.

We lay our trainers side by side. If it was Conor Corcoran he'd be making comments about the size of my feet by now. But Harry's not like that. We wobble our way to the centre and start bouncing.

'Well, come on then, sing!'

If anything, his voice is even worse: deeper now, but still so glass-shatteringly terrible that the only ones feeling the love in the air tonight are probably double-glazing salesmen.

'Okay, okay, stop, please. That's enough, Harry.'

'Told you I couldn't sing.'

But we carry on bouncing, so close that it's impossible to avoid the occasional meeting of random body parts – or maybe one of us has stopped trying.

Harry takes out his phone. 'Hey, Lauren, what's your number?'

'What do you want my number for?'

'In case I need to call you. Or the other way round, of course.'

'Why would I need to do that?'

'Any number of reasons – a fashion show disaster, you might need some advice on your terrible taste in music, or who knows, maybe you'll get this uncontrollable urge to hear me sing again.'

'Okay, fine, it's . . .' I call out my number.

Two seconds later my phone rings.

'Hi, Lauren.'

'You're an idiot.'

'Thanks a lot,' says Harry.

'What do you want anyway?'

'I was just thinking.'

'Don't do that – you might hurt yourself.'

'Yeah, funny.'

'So what can I do for you?'

'Well, it's . . .' He stops bouncing. Both of us wobble, but we don't fall down. 'It's half-term next week, Lauren. Would you like to . . . do something?'

'Eh?'

'We could go and see a movie – or you could come round mine if you want.'

'What do you mean, like . . . like a date or something?'

'*No*, yes . . . I mean, maybe, I don't . . .'

Tell me I'm wrong, but we're not talking 'just mates' here, are we? 'It's probably not a very good idea, Harry. You see, I'm not really ready to —'

I ought to feel flattered. Two guys have come on to me in the space of an hour. Unfortunately, it's a bit more complicated than that.

'Don't worry about it,' says Harry. 'There's no pressure or anything. I mean, we could just take it really slowly and . . . and see what happens.'

'Look, I've got to go,' I say, struggling out of the black netting and scrabbling around beneath the trampoline for my trainers. 'My dad's waiting. I'll see you around.'

'Wait a minute,' says Harry. 'I was only —'

Katherine says she's a far more tragic female role model than Lady Macbeth, but I've always had a soft spot for Cinderella. And that's who I feel like, as I limp across the lawn in only one shoe.

20

TEA IN A CHINA CUP

'Let's go round the back,' says Dad. 'I've got a key. No point ringing the bell. It's like trying to wake the dead.'

The TV in the 'parlour' is blasting out *Homes Under the Hammer*.

'Look at this garden,' says Dad. 'Your granddad would have a heart attack.'

'He did, didn't he – twice?'

'Maybe it's just as well,' says Dad, unlocking the French windows. 'According to him, the whole world was going to the dogs.'

'I know. He told me – more than once.'

'Are you coming in then?'

'Maybe I'll wait out here for a bit. She might not want to see me.'

'Of course she will. You read her letter.'

The question is, do I want to see her? 'You'd better make sure she hasn't changed her mind.'

'Fair enough.'

I circle the garden (round and round like a teddy bear) and try to get my head together.

Back in the house, Dad is screaming at Grandma.

'About an hour and a half, Mum . . . No, Mum, I was very careful, I always am . . . No, don't get up, I'll make it.' It's weird how his voice changes when he starts talking about me. 'She's outside . . . Yes . . . Yes, I . . . think so, much better . . . Of course she wants to see you, why wouldn't she?'

Five laps later, Dad appears at the French windows looking like a surly schoolboy. 'I'm going to tidy up out here. Why don't you pop inside for a chat?'

'. . . Okay.'

Dad steps into the fresh air; I step into the 1970s. At least it still smells nice – cherry cake and wood polish, not decaying old people.

The parlour door is open. I glimpse the white of Grandma's perm sitting in front of a pointlessly deafening subtitled telly. A surge of affection does battle with a tsunami of rage.

I take a deep breath before I step out in front of her. 'Hello, Grandma.'

'Is that you . . . Lauren?'

At least she remembered my name. 'Yes, Grandma.'

'Hang on a minute, I can't hear a thing,' she says, aiming the remote at a property developer. 'Bloody rubbish anyway. He paid eight thousand pounds for that kitchen and there was nothing wrong with the old one.'

'Oh, right.'

'Now, let's have a look at you.'

I thought about wearing my shortest skirt just to freak her out, but I've opted for jeans and my *Trust Me, I'm The Doctor* T-shirt instead. 'Hello, Grandma.'

Her glasses are about an inch thick. What big eyes she's got!

'Quite the young lady, aren't we?'

'Uh-huh.'

It already feels like one of those phone conversations where the sound keeps dropping out.

'So, how are you . . . Lauren?'

'How are *you*, Grandma?'

'Oh, you know, sitting up and taking punishment.'

'Right.'

More dead air.

'You'd better be Mother,' she says, nodding at the beanie-hatted teapot on the tray. 'I'm a bit shaky these days.'

I slip into the empty chair beside her and reach for the strainer.

'Milk first. You haven't forgotten, have you?'

'No, Grandma. I haven't forgotten.'

'Have a biscuit.' Four bleeding hearts lie in wait for me on a bone china plate. 'I got you your favourites – Jammie Dodgers.'

(Yeah, about ten years ago.) 'No thanks.'

'Looking after your figure, eh?'

'Uh-huh.'

111

The clink of cup on saucer and the ominous banging from the bottom of the garden can't disguise another gaping hole in the conversation. I check the room for elephants. At first it looks clean. There are photos of me and Tilda everywhere – on the beach, playing French cricket with Granddad, that year they took us on the Easter egg hunt. It's only when you look closer that the uncomfortable truth starts to emerge. Because whereas Tilda turns into the stroppy teenager we all know and love, it's like I never made it to puberty.

And that's when I lose it, jumping out of Granddad's favourite armchair and prowling the room like a claustrophobic alley cat. 'What am I even doing here?'

More tinkling teacups. 'I thought we could try to —'

'And why did you ask me in the first place? You're obviously regretting it.'

'Of course I'm not.'

'Yeah, right, that's why you've spent the last two years avoiding me.'

She looks about four sizes smaller these days, as if she's shrunk in the wash. 'It wasn't like that.'

'The stupid thing is I believed them at first.'

'Believed what?'

'All those pathetic excuses: Granddad wasn't up to visitors; you'd decided to spend Christmas in a hotel that year; it was too far on the train. But it didn't take me long to figure it out.'

'I'm sorry, Tiger.'

'Don't you dare call me that.'

'At least let me try and explain, pet.'

'You couldn't even be bothered to write.'

'I didn't know what to say.'

'Well, that's a first.'

Her sad smile is a mixture of black holes and yellowness.

'I thought you loved me.'

'I'll always love you,' she says angrily. 'I've loved you since the day your dad told me I was going to be a grandmother.'

'So why did you cut me off like that? How do you think that made me feel?'

Her swollen fingers contract round the arms of her chair. 'I didn't want to. Really I didn't.'

'Then why?'

'It was Don,' she whispers.

'Granddad?'

'You know what he was like. He was old-fashioned, even in 1957. He just couldn't understand what you'd done.'

'Okay, so if it was all down to Granddad, why did you ban me from his funeral?'

'I didn't . . . Not really.'

'You told Mum and Dad not to bring me.'

'I'm sorry, Lauren, I —'

'Tilda was there.'

'We thought she'd cope better. You'd had a lot on your mind.'

'That is bollocks and you know it.'

I've often wondered what it would feel like swearing at her: not half as good as I expected.

'Please, Lauren. Sit down and drink your tea.'

'Even people in prison get let out for funerals.'

She dabs her cheek with a tissue, wiping away a gobbet of moisture, not tears but that gooey stuff from her glaucoma treatment. 'I'm sorry, Lauren. That was your granddad too. He told me he didn't want you there.'

'But you could have talked to him, couldn't you? And then afterwards, when he was dead, you could have invited me, anyway?'

'There was no talking to Donald. Once he'd made his mind up about something he was like the Rock of Gibraltar. Even in the hospital, after his second do, he still kept on about it.'

'I thought Granddad loved me too.'

'He did. You meant the world to him. But he could never see beyond the —'

'You mean he had nothing better to do on his deathbed than plan the guest list for his funeral?'

'He was thinking of Auntie Dolly and his friends from the photography club.'

'What?'

'And you.'

'Eh?'

'He didn't want you turning into some kind of sideshow.'

There's a brief moment of calm followed by an after-surge of anger. 'You still didn't have to go along with it.'

'I know. But it's what I signed up for. Love, honour and obey. That's how it was back then.'

'You're joking, aren't you? Mum thought that was the funniest line in the whole wedding ceremony.'

'Maybe things are different these days. A young woman starting out now has so much more control of her life.'

'I don't know about that.'

'When I first met Don, I was working in a dress shop – assistant manageress. I loved that job. But as soon as we were married he made me hand in my notice. He didn't want the neighbours thinking he couldn't support me.'

'That is so messed up.'

'Don didn't see it that way. No one did. And he was a good man, Lauren. Like that advert, he did what it said on the tin. I'd made him a promise and I couldn't go back on it. But maybe I should have been stronger. Like you, Tiger.'

And this time they're real tears roller-coastering down her bumpy old face. 'Oh, my darling, I've been so worried about you. But your dad says things are looking better for you these days.'

'Yes, much better, thanks.' I perch on the side of her armchair, squeezing her hand and drinking in the comforting smell of oranges and her eau de cologne

'I'm sorry, Lauren. I've been about as much use as a chocolate teapot. I just wish I'd tried harder to understand.'

'It is kind of complicated.'

'So why don't you tell me everything? Please, Lauren. I'd really like to know.'

I start at the very beginning, when Tilda was a baby, figuring that if I take things slowly, it might just make sense. 'You remember how angry I used to get sometimes?'

'Do I ever,' smiles Grandma.

'I think that was because —'

'Sorry, Mum, could I borrow Lauren for a second?' Dad is standing in the doorway, every inch the insurance salesman masquerading as a handyman. 'I'm going to have to sort out the shed roof. And I need someone to hold the stepladder for me.'

Later, when Dad popped upstairs to 'fix' the curtain rail, I finally got half an hour alone with her to try to explain. I'm not sure she'll ever get her head around it, but at least I know she's making an effort, because after tinned-salmon sandwiches, lemon drizzle cake and *The Archers*, she presents me with a small black box.

'This is for you, Lauren.'

'What is it?'

'Have a look.'

Inside is a necklace with square pink stones separated by delicate white beads.

'It's art deco, isn't it?'

'I don't know about that,' says Grandma. 'And it's only glass, my lovely. But my mother wore it on her wedding day so it's part of the family history.'

'Are you sure about this, Grandma? What about Tilda?'

'You're my eldest granddaughter, you should have it.'

'Thank you, it's lovely.' And compared with the 1990s wedding dress that Mum is seriously expecting one of us to walk down the aisle in, it really is. But not half as lovely as hearing Grandma call me her eldest granddaughter and almost sounding like she's proud.

'Well, you might want it for dressing up.'

'I don't really do that any more, Grandma.'

'No, of course not. You're a lovely young woman now. So don't forget to send me an up-to-date photo.'

'I won't, Grandma.'

I have to admit I'm still a bit misty-eyed later when she waves us off with her stick from the front door.

'Cheerio, Mum,' bellows Dad. 'Take care of yourself. I'll see you at Christmas.'

I wave and wave like a five-year-old.

Safely back in cruise mode, Dad sticks on a Rolling Stones CD and attempts some geriatric headbanging. 'Well, that wasn't so bad, was it?'

'I suppose not.'

'And you'll come again sometime, won't you?'

'Yes, yes, I think I will.'

I've always thought that forgiveness was just a word that people use to make themselves look good. So I'm not saying that things will ever be the same between us, but I'm starting to understand why Grandma acted the way she did.

And something else is clearer too. It doesn't matter how

much you love someone, you shouldn't give them complete control of your life. Sooner or later, you've got to make some decisions for yourself. So I reach into my jeans pocket and take out my phone.

'Who are you texting?' asks Dad.

'Just someone from school.'

The headbanging stops. 'You are careful about who you give your number to, aren't you?'

'Yeah . . . course.'

'And you do remember what I said about being too trusting?'

'Yes, Dad. Look, there's nothing to worry about, okay?'

Well, nothing apart from getting the words exactly right. It's not too flirty, is it?

Want to do something tomorrow? Can I come round yours?
Lauren X

21

HAPPY HARRY

Only an expert in parental paranoia, like I am, could detect the note of panic in her voice. She reminds me of a shopping channel presenter – well dressed and friendly on the heavily mascaraed face of it, but you sense the desperation inside. 'Hello. You must be Lauren.'

'Yes. Hi.'

'Hurry up, Harry, your friend's here.'

There are probably a hundred and one questions she's dying to ask me. I'd put money on the top three involving sex, drugs and what my parents do for a living, but the rules of the game mean she has to play nice.

'Harry's just putting a clean shirt on. He won't be a minute.'

I didn't dress up, otherwise Mum would have been suspicious – although I did stop in the leisure centre toilets to slap on some concealer. Tilda gets to spend the whole day in Brighton with her new friends no questions asked; I get the third degree every time I leave the house.

'You found us all right then?'

They live on the top floor of some three-storey apartments near the park. There's a nasty prison-cell lift, but I took the stairs instead. 'Yes, fine, thanks. I've got Google Maps on my phone.' Why can't I stop talking? 'That's a lovely view of the garden.'

'We share it with the other flats, but sometimes in the summer the residents' committee organises a barbecue and we all . . . *Hurry up, Harry.*'

I'm not very good at this – meeting the parent/s. Then again, I haven't had much practice recently. 'That sounds really . . .'

'*So anyway* . . . I hear you and Harry are in the same English group.'

'That's right. And we're both helping out with the fashion show.'

'I expect you're one of the models, aren't you? I love those jeggings. They are jeggings, aren't they?'

'That's right.'

It's not fair really, because I still remember quite a bit about her. We haven't actually met before, but I know Harry's dad moved to Manchester with a kitchen designer, and unless his mum's changed jobs in the last four years she's a primary school teacher who really wanted to be a chef.

'And how are you finding it up at St Thomas's?'

'It's not too —'

'She's doing fine, aren't you?' says Harry, still buttoning

his shirt as he comes to my rescue. 'What's with all the questions, Mum?'

'We were just talking, weren't we, Lauren?'

'Uh-huh.'

'Harry said you're new to the area. Where did you live before?'

'Give her a break, Mum, she's only just arrived.'

'And what about your parents, Lauren – how do *they* like it here? Bit quiet I expect.'

'Tell you what, why don't you make a list of questions and I'll email them to her?' says Harry.

'Sorry, Lauren, I was only . . . Would you like a drink?'

'I'm fine, thanks.'

'Right, we're off to my room,' says Harry. 'To listen to music or something.'

'Okay then,' says his mum. 'But are you sure you don't want to watch telly in here? I'll be catching up with some marking so I won't disturb you.'

'We'll probably need the Xbox,' says Harry.

'Lauren doesn't want to mess about on your Xbox, do you, Lauren?'

'I don't mind.'

'Fair enough,' she says, stealing another glance at Harry. I've seen that look before. My mum does it all the time. It doesn't matter how long ago it happened, or how well they're doing now, if your kid's life turns to shit for a while, you spend the next hundred years reassuring your-self that it's not about to kick off again. 'Good, good . . .

121

Right, well, have a . . . great time and, er, nice to meet you, Lauren.'

'Yes, you too.'

Harry leads me down the corridor. 'That's the bathroom, that's Mum's room and there's a little office space next door. And this is me.' Is the estate-agent patter supposed to be funny or is he as nervous as I am?

His bedroom is pleasingly lacking in the teenage boy smells I always do my best to avoid. And ridiculously tidy – a picture of all four Beatles on a clutter-free chest of drawers, an IKEA bookcase (books, CDs and Xbox games in alphabetical order), a lonely laptop on a pine desk and Blu-Tacked above it a revision timetable for the mocks.

'I can't believe you, Harry.'

'What do you mean?'

'It's like an IKEA showroom in here.'

'Tidy bedroom, tidy mind.' He smiles, screwing his index finger into the side of his head and drooling like a cartoon lunatic.

'If you say so.'

'Which reminds me, this is for you.' He takes a plastic bag from the wardrobe and hands it to me.

'What is it?

'I was going to give it to you at school, but you might as well have it now.'

It's the trainer I dropped at Izzy's party. I don't know what I was expecting, but I'm kind of disappointed. 'Oh right, thanks.'

He flips open his laptop and brings up his Spotify play-list. 'You can sit on the bed if you like. I'll take the chair.'

'Sure I won't crease your lovely duvet?'

Harry grins. 'No, you're fine.'

At least his taste in music has improved. 'Sorry about the other night, running off like that. My dad was waiting in the car.'

'No worries,' says Harry. 'What made you change your mind?'

'About what?'

'About, you know, getting together now?'

'Well, there's no reason we can't be friends, is there?'

'You tell me, Lauren.'

'Like you said, we can take things slowly and see what happens.'

It's hard to tell if he's a bit pissed off or just relieved. 'Yes, yes, good idea.' He taps three times on each arm of the chair. 'So what do you want to do then? I suppose we *could* play an Xbox game if you like.'

'If you want. But nothing violent, okay?'

'How about *Pro Skater Four*? It's a skating game.'

'You amaze me.'

'It's really old, but it's a good game to start off with.'

'I could give it a try, I suppose,' I say, acting like I've never seen an Xbox before.

He takes two controllers from the top drawer of his desk and joins me on the bed. 'A is for jump and these other buttons are when you want to do tricks.'

'Okay.'

'First we have to choose the characters. I'll be Bucky Lasek and you can be Jamie Thomas.'

I prefer Bam Margera, but best to let it pass. 'Okay then.'

'Well, just free-skate for a bit while you get the hang of it. That's you on the left, the guy with the red bandana.'

'Nice.'

It's not fair really, because I know a lot more about him than he thinks he knows about me. So while I know not to wind him up by asking too much about his dad, *he* doesn't realise that my cousin Stewart spent practically the whole of a rain-soaked holiday in Cornwall forcing me to play this game. So after we've skated around the college campus for a while, I kind of forget I'm supposed to be crap at it and start pulling off some triple-kick tricks and jumping off the car park roof.

'That's really good, Lauren. You're a natural.'

When we started playing, there was an ocean of freshly laundered duvet cover between us. But the more we explore the tennis courts together, the more the scent of Calvin Klein overpowers the fabric conditioner.

'Do you believe in second chances, Harry?'

'What kind of question is that?'

'A pretty simple one really.'

Bucky Lasek takes another tumble; Harry turns and looks me in the eye. 'Well, yes, I do actually.'

'What?'

'Believe in second chances. Most of us deserve to get it right in the end.'

The next thing I know our legs are touching. Jeans meet jeggings and neither of us pulls away. And just when I get the feeling he's about to put his arm round me, he coughs like the audience member from hell at your favourite movie and jumps off the bed.

'Sorry, can we pause for a minute? I, er . . . I could really do with a drink. Can I get you anything?'

'I'm fine, thanks.'

'I won't be a sec then. I'll just go and fix myself a coffee.'

'Oh, yes, right. You do that. I'll see you in a —'

And while he's gone, I check the room for elephants. At first it looks clean: a couple of dodgy CDs perhaps, but nothing that would give the game away. But then I see it, partially concealed behind the dangling legs of the wooden frog on the middle shelf – a shoebox covered in Super Mario Bros wrapping paper. I know exactly what it is. Mine's better hidden than Harry's, but I've got one in my bedroom too.

No, don't, Lauren, you mustn't.

And for at least five seconds I resist the urge to ease it off the bookshelf and carry it across to the bed. And once I've got it there, it takes at least another five seconds before I decide to open it. The three words in blue magic marker on the lid – *HARRY'S HAPPY BOX* – are just far too enticing.

What's weird is that I could probably have predicted the entire contents: a can of Red Bull (strictly forbidden, 'typical H'), the sixth season of *The Simpsons* (the one with Lisa's Wedding), a deck of Pokémon cards, a photo of his mum with his older brother (Jon, is it? He's probably at uni by now), a limited edition of 'The Black Parade', a battered copy of *Noughts and Crosses* (his twelve-year-old dystopia of choice), a squeaky red nose and a resealable sandwich bag of gummy worms.

I take out a multicoloured gelatine invertebrate and hold it up to the light. But as soon as I hear his footsteps, I grab Harry's Happy Box and slip it back on the shelf. All that remains now is to destroy the gummy worm.

Who'd have thought that a mouthful of barely flavoured gelatine could be such a blast from the past? But not in a good way. All I can remember is how unhappy we were. Back then I found it almost impossible to cry, but these days it's as easy as breathing. Not angry tears exactly, more like big blobs of cryogenically frozen sadness.

And I'm crying so hard that I don't hear him come back. It's only when I feel his arm on my shoulder that I realise he's sitting beside me.

'What's the matter?' he whispers. 'Why don't you tell me, Lauren? Maybe I can help.'

'I'm sorry, I can't.'

'Okay, if that's what you want. Like I said, we can take it as slowly as you like.'

'. . . Thanks.'

'But please don't cry, Lauren. There's actually nothing to cry about.'

And I want to believe him, really I do.

NOVEMBER

If one gesture symbolises more poignantly than any other the hollowness of the school experience it is the cringeworthy hugging ritual now considered necessary when girls greet even the most casual of acquaintances. Phonier than their friendship bracelets, they mask their insecurities behind a shallow facade of intimacy.

Dido's Lament: 1,000 Things I Hate About School

22

ANOTHER BRICK IN THE WALL

This would be even better if I'd talked Tilda into changing her mind. It's Friday after school in the sports hall, and our first rehearsal with the music is going really well until the three teachers step onto the runway and Mr Catchpole freezes.

'Not there, sir,' says Magda, struggling as usual to hide her frustration. 'Don't you remember, you have to get right to the front before you start posing?'

Mr Catchpole waves his arms at Katherine and Grunt (her friend/boyfriend?). 'Stop the music please. I *said* stop the music.'

The sports hall falls silent.

Izzy jumps in before Magda can go off on one. 'Don't worry, sir, you're doing fine. We can try it again if you like.'

'It's not that,' says Mr Catchpole. 'It's the song.'

'What's the matter with it?' says Magda. 'Don't you like Pink Floyd?'

'The sentiment is completely inappropriate. Not only

that, it should be we don't need *any* education – which is clearly nonsense, otherwise you couldn't possibly tolerate such a glaring grammatical error.'

'So what do you want us to do?' says Izzy.

'Find something more suitable. What are we supposed to be wearing anyway?'

Harry's been practising his commentary. He reads directly from his notes: 'The staff are preparing for their big night out. Miss Hoolyhan is modelling a full-length taffeta ball gown with matching accessories, Mr Peel is looking cool as usual in brushed denim and a vintage *Axe Poll Tax* T-shirt, and Mr Catchpole is wearing grey flannels, a tweed sports jacket and a green paisley tie – perfect for the PSHE teacher about town.'

'Yes, thank you, Harry, I think we get the idea.'

'How about "Take a Walk on the Wild Side"?' says Mr Peel. 'I know it's a bit left field, but it's got the same subversive vibe you guys are looking for.'

'Or maybe something from *Oliver!*' says Miss Hoolyhan.

The sports hall falls silent again. Mr Catchpole grinds his teeth.

Conor Corcoran tries to lighten the mood. 'I like your moustache, miss. Didn't know *you* were growing one too.'

'Not now, Conor,' says Miss Hoolyhan. 'We're trying to decide on the music.'

The room erupts with a riot of 'helpful' suggestions.

All *I'm* worried about is the trail of eczema climbing my legs. There's never a good time for a flare-up, but the thought of parading down the catwalk in a yellow beach dress alongside Conor Corcoran's Speedos is enough to bring anyone out in a rash.

'Shut up!' screams Magda. 'This isn't helping, okay?'

'For heaven's sake,' says Mr Catchpole. 'This is your own time you're wasting.'

I sneak a secret glance at Harry. He sneaks one back. We've been taking things slowly – Ice Age slowly. Neither of us wants to go public yet, so we've been careful not to leave school together or sit at the same tables, and Mum thinks I've been 'hanging out' with my new friend Katherine, which she's obviously delighted about.

In fact, everything was going fine until the 'weirdness' started.

'All right, let's leave it there for today, shall we?' says Magda. 'But remember, guys, there's only a week until the big night, so if you're planning on having your hair done or any other beauty treatments, don't leave it too late.'

Katherine and Grunt stage a loud discussion about their up-coming Botox injections.

'I'll see you tonight then,' whispers Harry.

'Yeah.'

'You all right?'

I fight the urge to scratch. 'Yeah, course. I'll see you later.'

All I really want is to run home and slap some emollient on, but Katherine ambushes me on the way to my locker.

'George wants to know if you've done the slideshow yet.'

'Kind of. I've been getting some photos together on my portable hard drive.'

'There's not much time you know,' says Katherine. 'I suppose I could help if you like.'

'Yeah, fine, that'd be good.'

'What's the matter with you anyway? I thought fashion was your thing.'

'Sorry, I've had . . . stuff on my mind.'

Katherine smiles, like she thinks she knows something. 'You mean Harry, I suppose?'

'What? No. Why would you say that?'

'I may not be one of the beautiful people, Lauren, but I do know how these things work.'

'Well, you should do. I've seen you flirting with that Grunt guy.'

'Oh *please*,' says Katherine, the light in her eyes flicking on for a second.

'Are you two seeing each other or what?'

'We're not interested in your moronic mating rituals. It's a meeting of minds, not . . . you know.'

'You sure about that, Katherine?'

And suddenly she's all businesslike again. 'So when are we going to get these photos done?'

'I don't know.'

'Let's fix a time, shall we?'

'All right, all right. How about after school on Monday in the ICT suite?'

'I'll be there,' says Katherine, reaching back and playing

with her ponytail. 'And just so you know, Lauren, his name's not Grunt, it's George, okay?'

By the time I get to the lockers, the thought of a whole weekend away from St Thomas's Community College has *almost* put a smile on my face. And I'm looking forward to my date with Harry tonight, if it *is* a date. Holding hands for a few seconds is about as far as it's gone. Maybe if neither of us hits the garlic, our first kiss could be on the cards.

I unhook the padlock and pull open my locker. The ghost of my smile is spirited away.

Holy shit, not again.

A green scaly monster is baring its teeth at me. With his tail horribly mutilated and jaws smeared with blood (or wait, is that lipstick?), he fixes me with a grey beady eye and my heart stops dead in its tracks . . .

Three seconds later, it springs back to life again at twice the original speed.

And as soon as I rediscover the power of movement, I chuck the monster in my messenger bag with the others and start running.

23

SHOW AND TELL

A hooded black figure is chasing me across the courtyard. Unlike the star of some of my nightmares, this one can actually talk. 'Lauren, Lauren, wait!'

'What is it, miss?'

'There's nothing the matter is there? Only I saw you running down the corridor and you looked a bit . . . out of sorts?'

'Did I?'

Miss Hoolyhan hands me a tissue. 'You'd better have this. I think your mascara is running.'

I try to stem the tide, like the little Dutch boy who shoved his finger in the dyke. 'It was a bit hot in the sports hall.'

'Yes, yes it was rather,' says Miss Hoolyhan, tugging at the toggles of her cagoule. 'I tell you what, why don't you come back to the music block and cool down for a bit?'

And even I'm surprised by how meekly I follow. 'Okay then, miss.'

I gave up violin lessons in Year Seven so I've never been up here before. There's a long curvy corridor with fluorescent lighting and fading photos of the great twentieth-century composers on the wall. 'That's Shostakovich,' says Miss Hoolyhan. 'He was a qualified football referee.'

'That explains the little round glasses then.'

'What? Oh yes, referees are supposed to be short-sighted, aren't they? That's very good.'

She opens the door to a room full of keyboards and instrument cases. Somewhere in the distance, a certified sadist is strangling a clarinet. 'Take a seat, Lauren. I could make you some tea if you like – I've got herbal.'

'No thanks, miss.'

She sits on the front table, tapping out a tune on an imaginary piano. 'Do you remember what I said to you when you first arrived here?'

'Not really, miss.'

'I said I hoped you'd come and talk to me if you were ever worried about anything.'

'Oh yeah, I remember now.'

She swings her legs in time to the imaginary music. 'Now I could be wrong of course, but I get the feeling something's not quite right.'

'I . . .'

'Yes?'

'I think that . . .'

'It won't go beyond these four walls, I promise.' Miss Hoolyhan thinks for a moment. 'Well, not unless you're in some kind of danger that is.' She thinks again. 'You're *not* in some kind of danger, are you, Lauren?'

'I don't know.'

'What do you mean?'

'All I wanted was to be left alone.'

'It's been going well, hasn't it?' she says. 'I've been so impressed with the way you've handled things.'

'That's what I thought, until . . .'

'Until what, Lauren?'

If I say it, it will make it real. But I can't pretend any more. 'I think someone must have worked it out.'

'You mean?'

'Yes.'

'But how?'

'I don't know. But I keep getting these – I'm not sure what you'd call them – presents, I suppose.'

'What kind of presents?'

'Weird presents.' I unzip my Beatles messenger bag in preparation for the creepiest show and tell ever. 'They left this on my table before registration.'

'It's just a toy car, isn't it?'

'The Lamborghini LP640. But look – all the windows are broken and there's a dent in the roof.'

'I don't really think you should read anything into that, Lauren. It probably belongs to some unlucky Year Seven. I doubt very much it was meant for you.'

'That's not the only thing. Last week l found this in my bag.'

'A water pistol?'

'It's a replica of a Beretta 92F handgun.'

'Ah, no,' says Miss Hoolyhan, taking aim at Tchaikovsky. 'I think I can explain that one. Some of the Year Tens started bringing them in last summer. They didn't seem to understand how serious it was. I think *I'd* better have that, don't you?'

'All right then. But how do you explain this? I found it just now in my locker.'

'Now that *is* strange . . .' She runs her finger across its bumpy forehead. 'But boys do like dinosaurs, Lauren. My nephew has got dozens of these.'

'Yes, and how old is he? About seven?'

'Well, yes, but —'

'And look, its mouth is smothered in lipstick and they've hacked off its tail.'

'Maybe this one didn't have a tail.'

'It's an allosaurus, Miss. They definitely had tails.'

'So what are you trying to say?'

'This is how it started last time. Silly stuff to begin with. And then it turned nasty.'

'I think you might be overreacting, Lauren. We've had this sort of thing before at St Thomas's. In fact, a few years back, someone started leaving tomato plants in my pigeon-hole. I was quite rattled for a while. But it turned out Mr Willcock had the idea I was a keen gardener.'

'There's more to it than that. I've got a bad feeling about this.'

'You know what you're doing, don't you, Lauren?'

'What, miss?'

'You're catastrophising. You've had some . . . traumas in the past and you've got this unconscious expectation that you're doomed to carry on repeating them.'

'You sound like a psychiatrist, miss.'

She seems about to say something, but moves swiftly on. 'What I mean is that you shouldn't go reading too much into a few random incidents. Perhaps you could mention it to Harry.'

'What for?'

'I thought you two were seeing each other.'

'Why do people keep saying that?'

'So it's not true then?'

'No, no, we're just friends, that's all.'

'Well, whatever your "relationship status"' – she smiles at her deft use of contemporary jargon – 'it might be good to talk to someone your own age. He's a nice lad. I'm sure he'd put your mind at rest.'

'Maybe I will, miss,' I lie.

'You can always come to me, of course. But whatever you do, don't bottle things up. At least have a good old heart-to-heart with your mum.'

'I will, miss.'

Except I won't, of course.

24

BURNT HAIR AND BODY BUTTER

Mum sits on the end of the bed while I straighten my hair. I wish she'd go, then I could sort out my neck. But she insists on distracting me with random conversation starters that don't lead anywhere.

'I swear that damp patch is getting bigger.'

'Is it, Mum?'

'The surveyor didn't even pick up on it. How could anyone be so blind?'

I watch her in the mirror, wondering if a woman over forty should really be wearing a Disney sweatshirt.

'Looks like it's going to rain again – you'd better take an umbrella.'

'Yes, Mum.'

'If you wait for Dad to get home, he could give you a lift.'

'*No*. I mean, thanks anyway, but I'll be fine. It's not exactly a jungle out there, is it?'

'That's not the point, Lauren. A young girl like you

needs to be careful.' And she gives me 'the look'. 'You will take care of yourself, won't you?'

'Yeah, course.'

The headachy aroma of burnt hair and body butter competes with the dull throb of Tilda's baseline from the room next door.

'You're going to a lot of trouble for a girls' night in.'

'Katherine's a bit obsessed with her appearance,' I say, congratulating myself on a lie that's actually funny as well as practical. 'I thought I should make an effort.'

'I see,' says Mum. 'It's just that . . .'

Our eyes meet in the mirror. 'What?'

Her fake smile would look better on the catwalk. 'I'm so glad you're having such a good time at school.'

'Who told you that?'

'Tilda. She says you've been making new friends.'

'Oh, yes.' How would she know anyway? We've barely spoken since Izzy's party.

'That's right,' says Mum, rising slowly from the bed and joining me at the mirror. 'In fact, she said she thinks you . . .' Verbal constipation gets the better of her again. 'She thinks you might have started seeing someone.'

And suddenly I see where she's going with this. 'It's a school, Mum. I see a lot of people.'

'Don't try and be clever with me, Lauren. You know what I'm talking about.'

I turn to face her, hair straighteners raised in self-defence. 'Do I?'

142

'This boy – Harry, is it? – you're not dating, are you?'

Cue the sound of hair straighteners tumbling onto a frayed blue carpet.

'Sort of. I mean not dating exactly, but we have been seeing each other.'

'Oh, Lauren,' she says, screwing her face into a tragic mask. 'How could you?'

'I'm sixteen years old, Mum. What's your problem?'

'You know what my problem is.'

And guess what, I'm losing it again. 'Scared I'm going to get pregnant, are you?'

'Don't be disgusting.'

'Well, it's obvious you don't trust me.'

'Of course I trust you. I just don't want you to get hurt. And neither does your sister. She's almost as worried as I am.'

'I won't get hurt, Mum. Harry's a nice guy, I know he is.'

'Now where have I heard that one before?'

'Please, Mum, don't.'

She grabs her forehead and tries to rub away the wrinkles. 'Why didn't you tell me?'

'Because I knew you'd be like this?'

'Like what?'

'Frightened.'

'It works both ways you know, Lauren. You've got to trust me too – especially after everything we've been through together.'

'It's not that, Mum. I have to start making some decisions for myself.'

'And what about this Harry? He doesn't know, does he?'

I opt for the simple answer. 'No, Mum.'

'It's hardly fair on him, is it, Lauren?'

'What do you mean?'

'Getting close to the boy, if you haven't told him about . . . your past.'

'I'll tell him if things start getting serious.'

'Oh, good God.'

'Don't be like that, Mum. We moved here so I could have a normal life. You can't go all mental on me when it starts working out.'

'It's not that. I just worry about you. You've been so happy lately. What if this boy ruins everything?'

'He won't. I know he won't.'

'Well, you'd better not bring him round here. Not just yet anyway. You know what your dad would say.'

'I've got a pretty good idea.'

Mum cracks a knowing smile. 'There's not a father on earth who wants his daughter to grow up, Lauren – sons, yes; daughters, not so much.'

'So could you and Tilda keep quiet about it for a bit?'

'I'll have a word with her,' says Mum, picking my pants off the floor. 'No point worrying him just now. He was so pleased that you'd sorted things out with Grandma.'

'I wouldn't go that far. But at least we're talking again.'

Mum starts work on a pile of damp towels. 'So I assume that's who you're seeing tonight then. This Harry, I mean.' She braces herself for my reply.

'Yes.'

Mum's so much better at this than she was; the earthquake inside her registers only the hint of a tremor on her face. 'And where's he taking you – somewhere nice I hope?'

'*He's* not taking *me* anywhere. But we're going to Pizza Express.'

'Right, I think I've got a voucher somewhere. I'll print it out for you.'

'Thanks, Mum.'

'And don't walk back through the station subway, will you? Go the long way round. And before you ask, I said exactly the same thing to your sister.'

'Oh, come on, Mum. It's miles further that way.'

'That's what Tilda said.'

'You shouldn't worry so much. I'm a big girl now, you know!'

'Oh, come here,' says Mum, stretching out her arms and pulling me towards her.

I lay my head against Mickey Mouse and drink in the reassuring combination of coffee, hairspray and Anais Anais.

'I'm sorry if I'm over-protective sometimes. I can't help it. All I've ever wanted is for you to be happy.'

'I know that, Mum.'

She strokes my hair. I've always liked having my hair stroked.

'That looks nasty, Lauren.'

'What does?'

She pulls me sideways so I'm under the light. 'This eczema. You're not having another flare-up, are you?'

'It's just a tiny dry patch, that's all.'

'How long have you had it?'

'About a week. I've been using the steroid cream.'

'This isn't good.'

'Oh, Mum, please.'

And now the inevitable interrogation. 'There's nothing on your mind is there, my love?'

'Why should there be?'

'We both know what stress does to you. That is exactly what happened last year.'

Lucky I'm wearing jeans. She'd have a fit if she saw the back of my legs – but not half as bad as if I told her about that dinosaur.

'There's nothing to worry about, Mum. It's just this house. I think I'm allergic to something.'

And for some reason she chooses to believe me. 'I've got a nice silk scarf that will cover it up. It will go with your jeans too.'

And I thought my days of dressing up in Mum's clothes were long gone! 'Thanks, that's really nice of you.'

'Oh and, Lauren?'

'Yes.'

'I hope you don't mind me asking you this but —'
'But what, Mum?'
'You have been taking your medication, haven't you?'
'Of course I have. I'm not stupid you know.'

25

PIZZA EXPRESS

Three mouthfuls into the chocolate fudge cake, I start wondering what it would be like to kiss him.

'What are you looking at, Lauren?'

'Nothing, just the —'

'Have I got chocolate round my mouth?'

'Oh yeah, yeah, you have actually. Let me just . . .' I take a napkin, reach over the table, and run it slowly across Harry's top lip. It feels just as I imagined it, even down to the prototype bristles that he hasn't bothered to start shaving yet. 'That's better.'

His cheeks ignite for a second. 'Thanks. I'll ask for the bill, shall I?'

'We're not in a hurry, are we? You said you were going to tell me about your brother's new band.'

'It's fine by me, but I thought you said you had to be home by ten.'

'Oh yeah, that's right. Better get a move on, I suppose.'

It's hard to explain. It ought to be the exact opposite,

but whenever I'm with him I feel safe. And it's amazing how many things we find to talk about when so much is 'out of bounds'.

'I won't come to the door with you,' says Harry. 'Not if your dad's the monster you say he is.'

'He's just a bit, you know, protective. But that's okay, you can just drop me on the corner.'

'What do you mean "drop" you?'

'Aren't you going to give me a lift on your bike?'

'You are joking, I hope. I've haven't even got my full licence yet. And anyway, there's only one helmet.'

'We could cut through the park. No one will see us. Come on, it'll be a laugh.'

'I'm not breaking the law for a laugh, Lauren.'

'So what are you going to do with your bike?'

'I'll walk you home first and then come back for it.' He finally manages to attract the waiter. 'What are you laughing at?'

'You're such a yes man, aren't you?'

'No I'm not.'

'Oh come off it, Harry – you're bloody perfect, you know you are.'

'You think so?' he says, chasing a slither of strawberry around his plate.

'I know so. I mean look at you. Deputy head what-doyoucallit, captain of practically everything. I bet you've even started work on your CV.'

'Sorry I'm such a disappointment.'

'That's not what I meant, Harry. I really like it that you're so together. Not like me.'

The waiter plonks a silver saucer on the table. I grab the bill.

'You're doing all right, Lauren. Better than all right. We both are.'

And I suppose for two people with Happy Boxes in their bedrooms, he's probably right.

Harry breaks into a smile. 'Why do girls always do that?'

'What?'

'Add up the bill.'

'Because it's like being accused of a crime you didn't commit. We don't want to end up paying for something we haven't had.'

I take his arm and we walk back through town in the rain.

'I was talking to Miss Hoolyhan after the rehearsal.'

'Oh yes, what about?'

'Well, about you for a start.'

He checks his reflection in the Body Shop window. 'And the fashion show I suppose. It's not what I said about that new outfit they want her to wear?'

'No, she was just saying what a nice guy you are.'

'Did she?' he says, not sounding too thrilled about it. 'I'd have preferred "sex god", but you can't have everything I suppose.'

I don't have many hidden talents, but it turns out I can

do a great Miss Hoolyhan impression: 'And it wouldn't have been very "appropriate" either, would it, Harry?'

'No, miss!'

It's probably the perfect moment to wrap my arms round his neck and get that first kiss over with, except I'm about to ruin it all by asking the question that's been simmering in the back of my mind since we left Pizza Express.

'What did you mean just now?'

'Eh?'

'When you said we were both "doing all right". What were you talking about?'

'Well . . . school, of course,' he says, pausing for a moment in front of Marks & Spencer and tapping the top of his thigh. 'You're the star of the fashion show and I . . . well, I just got my Duke of Edinburgh Award. We could be like . . . you know . . . a power couple.'

'Oh . . . I see.'

We walk up to the station in silence. The announcer apologises for the late arrival of the 9.56 train to Victoria and we cut across the empty car park towards the subway.

'I'm supposed to go the long way round,' I say, trying to kickstart the conversation. 'My mum says someone was mugged down there.'

'Oh come on, Lauren, it'll take forever. And it's not like you're alone, is it? I thought *I* was supposed to be the yes man.'

'I didn't say I was going to do it, did I?'

'*Bloody* hell,' says Harry as we enter the subway. 'It's

worse than the reception-block toilets. Do you think graffiti artists have weak bladders?'

Half the lights are missing and it curves round to the right. So I don't spot him until we're halfway down.

'Oh my God, that's . . . horrible.'

'What is it?' says Harry. 'Is it the smell? You look like you're going to faint or something.'

'Down there – look.'

At first he seems as shocked as I am. And then, out of nowhere, he breaks into a deep, throaty laugh. 'Some people have the weirdest sense of humour.'

Hanging by the neck, from a green shoelace attached to a broken light fitting, is Woody from *Toy Story*, a goofy grin on his face. I race towards the swaying cowboy, removing his head from the homemade gallows, like he's a real person and there might just be a chance of resuscitating him. A quick examination reveals it's too late. So I stuff him into my coat pocket before Harry can check him over too.

'You should have left him up there,' says Harry. 'It's actually pretty funny.'

'No it's not.'

'At least he died with a smile on his face.'

'It's gross – a little kid might see it. And anyway it's evidence.'

'Evidence of what?'

'I don't know . . . vandalism.'

'There's no need to take it so personally.'

'Isn't there?'

'What are you talking about?'

But I can't reveal the results of my hasty post-mortem and the chilling epitaph scratched into the bottom of Woody's boots. On one foot are my initials, on the other the abbreviation RIP.

'Nothing; let's just go home, okay?'

Harry starts murdering 'You've Got a Friend in Me'. And now I feel like murdering him.

'Stop it, Harry! Don't be such an idiot.'

'I was only —'

'Just shut up. Okay?'

And somewhere between the station subway and next door's Vauxhall Meriva, I kiss goodbye to our first goodbye kiss.

'Better not come any further,' I say, checking the curtains for signs of maternal twitching.

'Do you want to tell me what happened back there?'

'Nothing. I —'

'Lauren, wait,' says Harry, his outstretched arm fluttering in the rain. 'There's something I need to tell you.'

But all I want is to get inside. 'Look, I'll see you later, yeah?'

26

SWEET DREAMS (PART ONE)

Mum's waiting for me at the door. 'So how did it go then?'

'Yeah, good thanks.'

'Thank heavens for that.'

'. . . Yeah.'

She looks down at the smiley cowboy peeping from my pocket. 'Well, that's nice – he bought you a present.'

'Oh, yeah, right.'

'Good choice too – you loved those films, didn't you? I don't know how many times we sat through them on DVD.'

'I'm off to bed, Mum.'

'Come and say goodnight to your dad first,' she says, raising a knowing eyebrow. 'He'll want to know how you got on.'

I pop my head round the door and fake a smile. 'Night night.'

Dad and Tilda are watching his new box set about some French kids who come back from the dead.

'How was your friend Katherine?' he says.

'Yeah, good thanks.'

'And what did you get up to?'

'Nothing much, just microwaved some popcorn and watched a movie.'

'Which one?'

'Er . . . *Toy Story 2*.'

'How sweet,' says Tilda sarcastically.

'I'm sorry, I'm really tired. I'll see you in the morning.'

Big Moe's still not picking up. So I re-examine Woody for more clues. And I'm so freaked out that when I pull the string in his back, I half expect him to name the killer. But he doesn't say a word – just smiles.

Harry texts me again. I don't text back.

All that's left is to smother half my body in emollient, struggle into my straitjacket pyjamas with the special mittens to stop me scratching and climb into bed.

I try to put it off as long as possible. I even flick through *Marie Claire* for a bit. But I know what's coming. No matter how hard I try to stay awake, eventually I'll close my eyes and I won't be able to open them again. And whatever anyone tells you, you can't control your nightmares. It's like watching a horror movie with your hands tied behind your back.

But maybe tonight I'll get off lightly, because the opening scene is more like a happy dream from my childhood. I mean, what's so terrible about lying in a bath of gummy worms? And although some people might find the white-faced clown hiding in the washing basket a touch disturbing, the clowns were always my favourite part of the circus.

When the gummy worms turn to snakes and the white-faced clown spits out a small boy carrying a Beretta 92F handgun who starts chasing me through a dark forest, it's business as usual. Hanging from the trees is a multitude of life-sized Woodys, not smiling but choking. And when I try to run, my feet sink further into the mud. But maybe I'm better off where I am because as the small boy with the gun closes in on me, I have this terrible feeling that whatever lies beyond the forest is even worse.

That's when the moaning starts: soft at first, and then suddenly louder, as if some crazed pensioner is in charge of the remote.

I try to scream. But someone's trying to suffocate me. All that emerges is a muffled cry.

'Shh,' says Tilda, removing her hand from my mouth. 'You'll wake Mum and Dad.'

'What happened?' I say, swiftly coming to my senses in a coating of sweat.

'You've been dreaming,' she said, tenderly unsticking some wet hair from my face. 'You sounded awful. Do you want me to get you a glass of water?'

'No, stay with me a bit.'

'And why are you wearing those pyjamas? You haven't got eczema again, have you?'

'It's nothing really.'

'This is what happened last time. Please tell me there's nothing bad happening.' For once she actually sounds concerned.

But I can't lie to Tilda. 'I don't know. Look, you won't tell Mum, will you?'

'Why not?'

'Because I'm not sure yet.'

It's only when my eyes become accustomed to the darkness that I see how terrified she looks. And I really wish I could find some way of consoling her. But she only says what we're both thinking.

'It's starting again, isn't it?'

27

PRIVATE VIEW

Just as I'm giving up on my cheese and tomato panini, I spot Harry at the canteen door. He usually goes for a table as far away from me as possible, so it's a surprise when he races over.

'I've been trying to talk to you all weekend. Why didn't you call me back?'

'I thought we weren't supposed to be seen together.'

'Sod that,' says Harry, taking the seat opposite. 'No one's looking anyway. And it was your idea to keep quiet about it.'

'You didn't take much persuading.'

'Never mind that. What have you been doing?'

Sitting in my bedroom while a plague of eczema crawls up my legs. But a girl never boasts about her skin complaints. 'Nothing. Just watching Netflix and catching up on that *Pygmalion* essay.'

'I thought we were going to do something.'

'Sorry, I forgot.'

'Have you been you avoiding me?'

'No.'

'This isn't something to do with that stupid *Toy Story* thing is it?'

'No.'

'Because you did go a bit mental.'

'Sorry, I just really love those movies. It was like seeing someone torturing your favourite puppy.'

A distant flame flickers beneath his corneas. 'That reminds me, Lauren, I want to show you something.'

'Okay, what is it?'

'Not here. You'll have to come and see.'

'Just let me finish my drink.'

He grabs my hand and drags me to my feet. 'Let's do it now. I really want you to see this. I think it might explain a lot.'

'Is it okay if I show Lauren my painting, miss?'

The lady in the green overalls beams at him like a long lost son. 'Yes, of course, Harry. You know where it is.'

'Thanks, Miss Gough.'

'I bet you're pleased with it, aren't you?'

'It's all right, miss.'

'Well, I think it's wonderful,' says the lady in green. 'If only some of the others were as self-critical as you.'

'It's in the store cupboard at the back,' says Harry. 'Come on, Lauren, I'll show you.'

I can't help smiling as he leads me past the gallery of

159

severed heads and dead rock stars. Because I'm taking mental bets on the subject of his painting – it's either a nice little watercolour of his moped or the town centre in the snow.

'Close your eyes,' he says, as he opens the door.

'Why, what for?'

'Just do it,' says Harry. 'There's something I want to tell you before you have a look.'

'Like what?'

He guides me into the store cupboard. 'Keep your eyes shut.'

'Okay, okay.'

The stench of PVA glue is almost overpowering. I watch the yellow patterns dance inside my eyeballs and listen to Harry breathing heavier than usual; he gulps in a mouthful of air and prepares to speak.

'I know you think I'm super together and everything, Lauren, but I'm not really. Not all the time anyway. And this is how I handle it, I —' He breaks off mid-sentence, like he's seen a ghost.

I'm – literally – itching to open my eyes. 'What's the matter?'

'Why have you started wearing trousers?'

'To hide my . . . Because it was really cold this morning.' I suddenly remember something Tilda once said. 'And equal opportunities and all that.'

'Right,' says Harry, tapping his foot on the cold stone floor. 'Anyway, what I'm saying is that if I'm ever feeling bad about something, stuff like this can help. It's a self-portrait by the way.' The tapping gets faster. 'It's okay, you can open your eyes now.'

My mouth falls wide open too. But the words don't follow.

If that's Harry's official self-portrait, what's the one in the attic like? Life-sized, but unlike any life form I've ever seen, it covers the whole of the back wall. At first it looks like the artist has paint-bombed his canvas with thick blobs of black and red. It's only when I step back a little that I see the pale blue eyes behind the blackness, following me round the storeroom like a screwed-up Mona Lisa. And that's when it hits me. This isn't a self-portrait of Harry, it's a self-portrait of H.

'What do you think of it?' he says.

'It's just like my nightmares.'

'Yes,' he whispers. 'Mine too.'

28

PLEASE LOOK AFTER THIS BEAR

All I want to do is go home. I'm more than a little weirded out by Harry's GCSE artwork and my skin is on fire. But Katherine kept hassling me about our 'important appointment in the ICT suite', so here I am at the slowest computer in the universe checking out possible photos on my portable hard drive.

'Sorry I'm late,' she says, planting a huge parcel covered in tacky snowman wrapping paper next to the monitor. 'But the good news is, someone's left you a present.'

'Well, you can take it away again.'

'That's funny,' says Katherine, checking out the Eiffel Tower photos on the monitor. 'I thought you were the kind of girl that loved surprises.'

'Where did you find it?'

'It was in our tutor base,' says Katherine. 'Don't thank me by the way.'

'So how do you know it's for me?'

'Because it's got your name on it,' says Katherine, pointing at the scrawly black writing on the label. 'L. Wilson. That is you, isn't it?'

'Who's it from?'

'How should I know? Probably one of your Year Seven admirers.'

'What admirers?'

'You really haven't noticed, have you? Some of that lot worship the runway you walk on.'

'Do they?'

She doesn't sound too happy about it. 'I've been at this school nearly five years now, and there are kids in my own tutor group who don't know my name.'

'I'm sure most of them do.'

'I couldn't care less,' says Katherine unconvincingly. 'What could I possibly have in common with any of them?'

'Maybe more than you think.'

'Thanks, Lauren, but even if that's supposed to be a compliment, we both know it isn't true. Now, why don't you open it, and then we can crack on.'

'Forget it. I don't want to.'

'Oh come on, someone obviously went to a lot of trouble with that.'

'Look, if you're so desperate to open it, be my guest.'

She's always reminded me of one of those kids who stopped believing in Father Christmas long before everyone else, and never more so than as she picks half-heartedly at the Sellotape. 'So what have we got here then?' It's a brown cardboard box. Katherine pulls back the flaps and peers inside. 'Well, that's a bit boring.'

'What is it?'

She reaches down and pulls out Paddington Bear, complete with red wellingtons, a blue duffle coat and a brown suitcase. 'Some people are so unimaginative.'

I could almost kiss the bloody thing. 'I think he's quite cute actually.'

It's only when the fake blood starts dripping onto the keyboard and she turns Paddington over that we see the knife in his back.

'Now that's more like it,' says Katherine.

'I can't believe anyone would do something like that!'

She looks at me like *I'm* the crazy one. 'You are kidding, of course?'

'What do you mean?'

'This is a school, Lauren. No one needs a reason to do anything.'

'It's just so unfair.'

'You pretty girls amaze me, you really do.'

'Eh?'

'You have it so easy.'

'That's not —'

'You swan around the school like you own the place. You expect everyone to bow down before your beauty and if the tiniest thing goes wrong in your life you have a nervous breakdown.'

'You don't know anything about me.'

'It's probably someone who's jealous of you and Harry. And I'll tell you another thing: if you let them get to you, it'll only end in tears.' But her voice softens when she sees I'm crying already. 'Let's press on with these photos, shall we? George had this great idea. When Magda walks down in hot pants to that Queen song, we should put up some pictures of steam trains.'

'Why?'

'Because it's genius,' says Katherine, sounding more like her new boyfriend/guru every day. 'Come on, let's get it over with.'

'I'll do it at home,' I say, ejecting my hard drive and stashing it in my messenger bag. 'I can't stay here.'

'Yes, that's right. There's obviously a serial killer on the loose.'

'It's not funny, okay?'

'I know,' she says, her bottom lip trembling satirically. 'How many more innocent toys will have to die?'

'I'm out of here. I'll see you tomorrow.'

'Typical,' says Katherine. 'What exactly is the *matter* with you?'

'You don't want to know.'

'What shall I do with Paddington? Do you want me to look after him?'

'Yeah, funny.'

And she can't resist throwing in some final words of wisdom. 'It'll only get worse if you show them they've won.'

29

SWEET DREAMS (PART TWO)

Mum and Tilda are watching *Don't Tell the Bride*.

'God that's disgusting. I'd rather die than get married in a hot-air balloon.'

'Yes, but the wedding ceremony only lasts an hour. Marriage isn't about winning one battle, Tilda. It's about winning the war.'

I sit at the lounge table with a pile of papers and my laptop in front of me, trying to match photos to the music and outfits. It's not exactly rocket science (or even GCSE food tech) but I'm getting nowhere fast. This was supposed to take my mind off things, but all I can think about is a bear with a knife in its back and a label with my name on it.

What does it all mean anyway? Even Sherlock would struggle to make sense of a trail of mutilated toys. So I'm doing my best to see it like Miss Hoolyhan – that it's just a random St Thomas's kid with a warped sense of humour.

Or maybe Katherine's right and it's someone with the hots for Harry.

But what if it's more than that? What if . . . ? I can't tell Harry, Big Moe's obviously on strike or something, and I know for a fact it would scare the hell out of Mum. Even back in the Dark Ages, I never felt more alone.

When the Eiffel Tower turns into Paris in the rain, I realise I'm crying – silently so I don't disturb Mum. But she must have some kind of sixth sense because the next thing I know she's standing over me with a box of tissues and a mug of tea.

'There you go,' she says, putting down a coaster first. 'You look like you could use it.'

'Thanks, Mum.'

She leans down and kisses the top of my head. 'Is this something to do with Harry?'

'No, Mum.'

'Because no boy is worth it, Lauren, take it from me.'

'It's not about Harry, Mum.'

'Well then, what is it, my love?'

'It's this fashion show.'

She tries to censor herself, but it just slips out. 'I did say it might be too early for you, didn't I? Do you want me to talk to Mr Catchpole?'

'It's not that, Mum. I said I'd do this kind of back-projection thing. But the show's next Friday and I haven't even started yet.'

'Next week, is it? I'd better tell your dad so he can get off work early. I know he'll want to be there,' she adds doubtfully.

'Why am I so *useless*?'

'You're not useless, Lauren. You've just had a lot on your mind.'

'Like what?'

'Well, like starting a new school and everything.'

'Yeah, I *suppose*.'

Mum glances across at the bridesmaids in their Storm-trooper outfits. 'Tilda's good at that sort of thing. Maybe she could help.'

'I don't think she —'

'Tilda, come and help your sister with this.'

'Do I have to? What is it anyway?'

'She wants a hand with her computer thing for the fashion show.'

'I'm watching this.'

'Well, pause it and come over here. Your sister needs you.'

'*Okay*, I'm coming,' says Tilda, freezing the bride in the middle of her *Star Wars* themed reception rant. 'I have got a life too, you know.'

'I'll leave you to it,' says Mum, edging away. 'You don't mind if I watch something else, do you?'

'So what's the problem then?' says Tilda, thawing a little when she sees my face.

'I'm making a slide show. There's the track list, here's

a list of the models and that's what we're wearing. And I've downloaded about a million photos.'

'Right,' says Tilda. 'So what have you got so far?'

'Not a lot really; just some pictures of, like, posh houses for the prom dresses.'

'Sweet,' says Tilda, starting to click through my photo gallery. 'So how about this one of the wind farm for the Year Seven recycling project?'

'Good idea.'

Tilda looks down the cast list. 'Oh no, you're not, are you?'

'What?'

'Modelling beachwear with that dickhead Corcoran?'

'He's not that bad really. And anyway, I'm not wearing a bikini or something tacky – just a cute little beach dress.'

'Well, at least you're doing it to your favourite song. Maybe you could use that picture of Brighton Pier.'

'You mean the one with the helter-skelter?'

'Yeah. And you know the autumn collection – how about this photo of New England in the fall? That's what they call autumn in the States, isn't it?'

'Uh-huh.'

After that Tilda more or less takes over, which is a real relief, I don't mind telling you. She was always way better at this kind of stuff. But just as I'm starting to feel more optimistic she lowers her voice to a concerned whisper. 'What were you really crying about?'

'Like I said, the fashion show.'

'Has something happened again?'

'No . . . no . . . I don't —'

'Because the other night you said that —'

But I don't want to frighten Tilda either. 'It was just some silly stuff at school. Honestly, Tilds, I thought it might be . . . significant, but it *wasn't*.'

'You would tell me, wouldn't you?'

'Yeah, course,' I lie.

'Mum told me to keep quiet about you and the prefect guy. What's that all about?'

'You know what Dad's like. He'd have a fit if he found out.'

Tilda nods and almost smiles. 'But what does Mum think?'

And if I'm not *completely* honest, it's because I genuinely believe that if she wasn't shit-scared of it all kicking off again, it's the kind of thing that Mum would probably want to say. 'She's really happy for me. She says it's about time I got on with my life.'

'Right,' says Tilda, bringing up a photo of the Tower of London. 'Well, that's good then.'

'Yes.'

'And you're definitely going ahead with the fashion show?'

And if I wasn't shit-scared myself, this is the kind of thing that *I'd* probably want to say: 'Yeah, course. I'm looking forward to it.'

*   *   *

170

It's late by the time we finish uploading the photos. I didn't want to go to bed anyway, but in the end there's nowhere left to hide.

I find it kind of challenging, looking at my naked body in the mirror. I'm getting better at it, but there's still no 'girlfriend, you look amazing!' for me, just a tsunami of self-doubt. But tonight it has to be done. I need to check out my eczema. And there are traces of it everywhere: round my neck, my wrists, my elbows, across the back of my hands and down into my most private places. I'll tell you one thing: it's going to take a shedload of concealer to get me down that runway.

What I really need is a good night's sleep. Like that's ever going to happen. The moment my head hits the pillow I get this horrible feeling that I've been here before.

There's only one thing worse than a regular nightmare and that's the kind of nightmare where you know you're dreaming but you still can't wake up. And by now, I know what's coming. It's been variations on the same theme since Friday night. Only this time it's not a small boy with a handgun chasing me, it's a bear in a blue duffel coat who jumps out from behind a tumbledown ring of gravestones and threatens me with a knife. And here I am again, stumbling through the forest, slowly suffocating as I sink further into the mud.

The bear snarls. I drag my feet towards him, figuring that whatever he's got in store for me isn't half as horrible as the hidden menace beyond the woods. But what could possibly be that terrifying? And while every bone in my body is screaming 'Don't do it', another force is twisting my neck round and forcing me to look.

All I can make out are four white letters on a pale blue background:

KILL

And to be honest, it's better than I'm expecting. It's only when I pull aside the sopping branches and read the sign in full, that it all makes sense.

OAKHILL HOUSE

30

FINAL COSTUME FITTING

Second break on Thursday and that bloody clarinet still isn't dead.

'I feel like Miss Havisham.'

'Like Miss who, miss?'

'It doesn't matter,' she says, studying herself in the mirror we lugged up from the staffroom.

I'm not sure whose idea her new outfit was, but Miss Hoolyhan really ought to have told them to sod off. 'I think it looks all right, miss.'

'It's probably the only time my mother will get to see me in a wedding dress. Mind you, I think she'd be happy if I walked down the aisle in a black bin liner.' She tries to put a brave face on it, but she's not smiling inside. 'So, anyway, Lauren, are you looking forward to tomorrow night?'

'I'll be glad when it's all over to be honest.'

'Well, you've done a great job with those photographs. That slide show's going to work beautifully.'

'It was my sister really. She had all the ideas.'

'And what about the . . . other thing? How are you feeling about that?'

'I've been trying not to think about it. And at least no one's left me another "present" for a while.'

'That's good then,' says Miss Hoolyhan, playing peek-a-boo with her veil. 'Perhaps you won't have any more trouble.'

'I hope not, miss.'

'You really shouldn't go jumping to conclusions, you know. I hate to admit this, but there's bullying in every school. And most of the time there's no rhyme or reason for it.'

'That's what Katherine said.'

'Yes, well, she probably understands these things better than most. I thought you two would be good for each other. She's really been looking out for you, hasn't she?'

'Yes, miss . . . and thank you, miss.'

'What for?'

'For letting me try my outfits on up here, and being so cool about things.'

'You deserve to be happy, Lauren,' she says, sneaking another look in the mirror. '*Right*, I'd better get out of this thing before I start getting attached to it.'

'At least you've had a career, miss. Not like my grandma.'

I was trying to make Miss Hoolyhan feel better, but I'm guessing from the look on her face that comparing her with Grandma has only made things worse. 'I've laid out your outfits in order, Lauren. Starting with the beach dress. Any problems, give me a shout. Otherwise leave them where they are and I'll take them back to the sports hall after school.'

The blushing bride gathers up her train and heads for the door.

And I'm kind of looking forward to the next part. The yellow beach dress is a touch on the short side, and a bit see-through in places, but it will cover the worst of my eczema and it's actually pretty cute.

I hold it up to myself, the happiest I've felt in front of a mirror for weeks. But when I start parading down the imaginary catwalk to the imaginary song in my head, a glossy photo of a familiar big-eared duo falls at my feet.

I reach down to pick it up, fearing the worst. Only this time I needn't have worried. It's a good luck card. Miss Hoolyhan must have left it. Wallace and Gromit are saluting me with a wide-eyed thumbs up.

And then I look inside.

Oh.
God.

So that's it then. My brave new world is officially over. It's time to face the music and – do what exactly? Well, no more lying to myself for a start. No more denying what I think I always knew. The writing is so awful it looks like the author used the wrong hand. But no matter how long I stare at it, the meaning is clearer than a Photoshopped supermodel's complexion.

Why don't you tell them what you did to Luke?

31

ANGER MISMANAGEMENT

Even I'm surprised by the intensity of my anger. White hot and bursting with destructive energy, I haven't felt this way in nearly half a decade. All that counselling should have wheedled it out of me. Perhaps it only forced it deeper into hiding.

Last year, the best I could manage was neutered self-pity; this is the kind of undiluted rage that no anger-management technique on earth could contain. So instead of counting to ten, taking deep breaths or drinking a glass of water, I storm out of the music block with only one thought on my mind: squeezing a confession from the prime suspect.

'It was you, wasn't it?' I say, vaulting the steps of the Millennium Pagoda and stabbing an accusing finger at Katherine.

'You've all met Lauren, haven't you?' she says. 'There's obviously something on her mind.'

'Don't play games with me.'

'I loathe games, you should know that.'

'Who told you anyway? And why did you do it?'

A confederacy of nerds looks anxiously up from their chess boards/iPhones/Sherlock Holmes anthology.

'Why did I do what?' says Katherine.

'You said yourself it was someone who was jealous of me and Harry. Well, no one else knows about us. And it's obvious you fancy him.'

'Oh for goodness' sake.'

I wave the Wallace and Gromit good luck card in her face. 'So I suppose you don't know anything about this?'

'I've sat through it at Christmas a few times. But to be honest, crudely animated anthropomorphism isn't really my style.'

I feel like punching her, but that's not my style any more either. 'And how did you even know about it? Who told you – was it Hoolyhan?'

Katherine puts down her sandwich. 'I wish you'd tell me what I'm supposed to have done.'

'Why couldn't you come straight out with it? Why did you have to frighten me like that?'

'Wait a minute. This isn't something to do with that bear, is it?'

'I should have known I couldn't trust a weird cow like you. And your blog's shit, by the way.'

The boy who claims to read fiction for pleasure, but never speaks, lets out a nervous giggle.

'Typical, isn't it?' says Katherine. 'Whenever there's trouble in paradise it's always one of us that gets the blame.'

'Pretty convenient, wasn't it?' I say, folding my fingers into a fist, 'that you should just *happen* be the one who found it.'

Katherine laughs. It's a strange mechanical sound, almost like they're muscles she's never used before. 'You have heard the expression "Don't shoot the messenger", I suppose?'

'*How many more innocent toys must die*, that's what you said. Well, that proves it, doesn't it? You must have known about the others.'

'Other what?' says Katherine.

'As if you didn't know.'

And there's a real danger that I might resort to violence again, when another unfamiliar sound takes us all by surprise. The boy who claims to read fiction for pleasure looks up from his Kindle and speaks.

'Can I say something?'

It's so unexpected that I let him continue.

'I have no idea what this is all about, Lauren. But whatever you're blaming Katherine for, it's pretty obvious that she didn't do it.'

'You reckon?'

'I'm not saying it's always for the best, but the one thing I do know about her is that she never tells a lie, not even to spare your feelings – *especially* not to spare your feelings. So if she says she's got nothing to do with it, then she's telling the truth.'

It may not be the kind of Sherlock Holmes-type brilliance

that some of them were expecting, but the terrible thing is, I know he's right. I just didn't want to believe it. Because the moment I manage to count to three, the explanation is so obvious even a psycho like me can't pretend any more. There's only one person it *could* have been.

'You bastard.'

Harry takes one look at me, dumps the rest of his pasta on the tray and heads for the door.

'Don't you dare walk away from me.'

'Let's take this outside, shall we, Lauren?'

'Why did you do it?'

'Not here,' he says, ploughing through a babbling bunch of Year Sevens.

'Why not?' I say, struggling to keep up with him. 'Ashamed, are you?'

'No,' says Harry. 'But you're obviously angry about something and I don't want you to make a fool of yourself.'

'You've done that already. How could it get any worse?'

But he doesn't stop until we're practically in the car park. His fake look of concern is positively putrid. 'Okay, Lauren, what's the problem?'

'I thought you actually liked me. Why would you lead me on like that?'

'I do like you. I thought that was obvious.'

My fist tightens again. 'Well, you've got a funny way of showing it.'

'I wish you'd tell me what you're talking about.'

'You can drop the act, okay? I know it was you that sent them.'

'Sent what?'

'Oh come off it. Why were you so keen to go through the subway? I wanted to go the long way round, but you weren't having it.'

'Are you still talking about that *Toy Story* thing? Look, if something's upsetting you, Lauren, I want to know.'

'Don't play the innocent. All those times when you tried to squeeze it out of me. And what about that weird painting of yours? I wasn't sure at first, but the message in the card proves it. It couldn't be anyone else, could it? We're the only ones who know.'

His face is as pale as the day we first met. And someone must have pressed the mute button, because when he opens his mouth, no sound comes out.

'Let's get this over with, shall we, "Harry"? What are you going to do next?'

'What do you mean *next*? I haven't done anything.'

But my mind is already flicking through the horrors to come. 'Tell the others, I suppose.'

'I'm not going to tell anyone anything.'

'Well, who gives a stuff anyway? I won't be sticking around to find out.'

'Where are you going?'

'Anywhere but here,' I say, turning and heading towards the gate.

He grabs my arm.

'Don't touch me.'

'You can't just walk out of school in the middle of the day.'

'Just you bloody watch me, H.'

32

LAST ORDERS

Was there ever a more depressing emotion than hope? Because now I think about it, it's the only thing that's kept me going for the last three months: the blindingly stupid idea that it was the start of something good; the crazy belief that I could be who I wanted to be and the world would let me get on with it.

Of all the schools in all the towns, I had to walk into that one. The past might be another country, but they've put up *Wanted* posters and confiscated your passport, and every time you step across the border the armed guards arrive to drag you back.

I'm not even crying any more, anaesthetised by the knowledge that it's game over and there's no point. In a perfect world I'd run straight home and spend the rest of the year in bed. But that would mean breaking the news to Mum. So I carry on walking.

Somewhere south of Waitrose car park, I slip on my shit-tinted glasses. And I see what a crap town it is. Crap shops, crap fake cobblestones, crap chuggers, crap band-stand, crap *Big Issue* seller, crap bloke outside Specsavers handing out crap adverts for crap half-price eye tests and crap fat ladies with their crap fat dogs. But you know what really does my head in? If it wasn't for me, my family wouldn't even be here. All that shit I've put them through was for nothing.

And Big Moe's *still* not answering: 'Just call me back, okay? What's the matter with you? You said you'd always be there for me. So just bloody pick up.'

'Watch where you're going, young lady.'

'Oh sod off, you miserable git.'

Two cans of Red Bull from the poundshop later, I'm buzzing again, auto-piloting through town and up the hill towards the roundabout, past Izzy's house where I have a sickening flashback to that party, and round one side of the nature reserve (*shut up, you stupid ducks*) until I come to the main road at the top.

Who cares if running across dual carriageways is gener-ally considered inadvisable? And you can pump your horns all you like because I don't give a toss. Like a million chickens before me, all I'm interested in is getting to the other side – which is pretty bonkers when you consider that I don't even know where I'm going.

And here's another first. In fact, it's so high up the parental list of forbidden practices they haven't even bothered to warn me about it. All the same, I pick a spot on the hard shoulder, summon up my best catwalk smile and stick out my thumb. The cooler the car, the bigger my smile, so I have to admit I'm a tad disappointed when a blue Peugeot 107 pulls up beside me and the window slides down.

'What on earth are you doing?'

I suppose I should be relieved it's a woman's voice. But you know what? I just don't care any more. 'Hitching a lift, what does it look like?'

'Have you any idea how dangerous that is?' says the voice.

'It's fine. I've done it loads of times.'

'I hardly think so. But if you have, it was extremely unwise.'

'Look, are you going to give me a lift or not?'

'You shouldn't be out here in the first place. A girl your age should *not* be hitch-hiking.'

'Okay, fine. But if you don't pick me up someone else will.'

'Now listen to me, I —'

It's probably the medication, but these days I can more or less cry to order. Maybe a few tears will do the trick. 'Please. I missed the bus. There's only two a day. I'm really late. And if *you* take me I'll be safe, won't I?'

The voice – reluctantly – relents. 'I'm going as far as Wivelsfold. Is that any help?'

'Great, thanks,' I say, opening the car door and jumping in.

'Don't forget your seat belt,' says the voice. 'The roads are full of lunatics these days.'

'I know what you mean,' I say.

The car picks up speed, but not a lot. I fix my eyes on the road, terminally frustrated by the driver's stubborn refusal to break the speed limit. And I'm not the only one with a death wish. The guy in the BMW M3 Saloon behind gets so fed up with tailgating that he screeches past us round the corner, miraculously avoiding the biker coming the other way.

'Shouldn't you be at school anyway?' says the voice.

'We've got the afternoon off. There's an open evening tonight.' It's a well-known fact that people love fairy stories – it's the first one that comes into my head. 'So I'm . . . going to visit my grandmother.' (*She lives in a cottage in the woods.*)

'And she's expecting you, is she?'

'Yeah, course.'

'Well, if I was your gran, I'd be worried sick.'

'It's lucky you're not then.'

'Someone needs to talk some sense into you.'

I sneak a proper look at her. It's hardly a revelation that she's ancient: yellow teeth, grey hair, black leather gloves and a red hairy growth on her cheek. She's obviously the kind of old person who thinks that having lived fifty years longer than me gives her the right to start handing out advice.

'And next time make sure you don't miss the bus.'

'Uh-huh.'

At least she doesn't go off on a three-hour lecture about

the British weather when the rain kicks in, she just turns on the windscreen wipers and sticks her nose up to the window. But as the dual carriageway becomes a winding single lane and we chug deeper into the countryside, she glances sideways and catches my eye.

'So where does she live then?'

'Eh?'

'Your grandma. Where would you like me to drop you?'

And to be honest (literally *and* metaphorically) I haven't a clue where I'm going. I'm so pissed off with everything I just need to get away. 'It's a few miles yet,' I improvise. 'I'll give you a shout when we're nearly there.'

'Yes, you do that,' says the old woman doubtfully.

I peer through the rain-spattered window, trying to get some idea of where we're headed. Set back from the road is a small white church surrounded by a zombie village of gravestones. Pinpricks of eczema lay siege to the back of my ankles and I get this uncontrollable urge to scratch.

The old woman flicks on the news: the posh version with the plummy voice. I keep my ears open for any juicy stories about missing schoolgirls, but I doubt they've even noticed I've gone. All we get are lying politicians and disgraced 1970s TV presenters. And when the plummy voice moves on to the price of petrol, the old woman reaches for the off switch.

Twenty awkward minutes later, she clears her throat. 'If there's anyone you want to call – your parents perhaps – I keep a mobile telephone in the glove compartment.'

'It's all right. I've got my own phone, thanks.'

'Of course you have.'

'I'll text my mum when I get to Grandma's.'

'Yes, well, make sure you do.'

'I will, I promise.'

An uneasy silence descends once more, punctuated only by the whirr of the windscreen wipers. Every few minutes the old woman takes a raspy breath, threatens to say something, and then thinks better of it. Eventually she speaks. 'I'm Jean, by the way.'

'Oh . . . right. I'm Lauren.'

'What a lovely name.'

'Thank you.'

'If there's something you're worried about, Lauren, you could always tell me, you know. I've got four grandchildren of my own.'

Is there anything more tear-jerking than the kindness of strangers? 'That's . . . great . . . Jean, but I'm fine, honest.'

'It's not about school, is it? There's a lot of pressure on you youngsters these days.'

Part of me would like to tell her everything. What a story that would be for her grandchildren! But I don't of course. 'I told you. I'm going to see my grandmother.'

'If you say so, dear.'

Half a netball match further down the road, we pass a pub called the Last Orders. There's a play area in the garden with a slide in the shape of a white-faced clown.

The pinpricks of eczema become a thousand daggers. Because that's when it finally hits me: this isn't some kind of random mystery tour – I know *exactly* where I'm going.

'I think we're nearly there,' I say, wondering why it's taken me this long to figure it out. 'About five more minutes.'

'Really?' says the old woman. 'It looks like the middle of nowhere.'

She's right. But I'm pretty confident I know where we are. And if I cut across the fields and approach it from the back there's less chance of being spotted.

And sure enough, fifty metres beyond a trio of tiny cottages and a barn conversion is an empty car park with spaces for about four cars.

'That's my grandma's house,' I say. 'The one in the middle. Can you pull in here, please?'

Jean slows to a snail's pace, checks the mirror three times, indicates for the benefit of the dead badger, and pulls up in front of the rusty pay-and-display machine. It seems impossible, but somehow her wrinkly face gets even wrinklier. 'It's getting dark. Maybe I should see you to the door.'

'*No*, it's fine. It's just back there. And you don't want to get wet, do you?'

She stares out at the teeming rain. 'You will be all right, won't you, Lauren?'

'Yeah, course.'

'Well, at least take my husband's mackintosh. You'll catch your death.'

I'd kind of imagined her as a lonely old lady. 'He'll need it, won't he?'

'I've been trying to get him to take it to Oxfam for years. You have it; you'll be doing me a favour.'

I reach into the back for the disgusting old raincoat. It stinks of dog. And I'm all for dumping it until I step out into the pouring rain. 'Thanks for the lift, Jean. And don't worry, I'll be okay.'

She calls after me. I catch the gist (something to do with always respecting myself and staying safe) but most of it is carried away on the wind.

I nod and wave, before walking slowly towards the row of cottages. Jean performs a torturous sixty-four point turn, and I glance back as she heads off down the road.

A moment later, I race back to the car park and set about trying to find the public bridleway sign that I know for a fact is lurking in the undergrowth.

And once I find it, I pull up the collar of this pervy raincoat, point my nose in the right direction and pray there are no mad cows about – apart from me! At least it's not far now: just a short walk across the field and the last part through the woods.

My feet sink into the mud, coating the bottom of my school trousers in a thick layer of goo. And by the time I hit the woods, darkness is closing in around me. But already I feel calmer, kicking through a carpet of soggy leaves.

And through the branches, I get my first glimpse of it, glowing gently like a child's night light, the usual cluster of teenage smokers huddled round the door. Behind them is a sign I can't read yet – white letters on a pale blue background that spell out the words:

OAKHILL HOUSE

33

SOMEWHERE ONLY WE KNOW (PART ONE)

The sign outside the door gives no clue to the building's purpose. Not even a logo or a simple *CAMHS in-patient unit* – just two words on a pale blue background.

It's kind of ironic, because a short walk down the hill is the yellow-bricked Victorian monster that they converted into a hundred luxury apartments when the new hospital was built. The foundation stone at the front entrance rather gives the game away:

COUNTY BOROUGH LUNATIC ASYLUM
– ESTABLISHED 1861

But if you check out the website – which I do sometimes, believe it or not – you'll see that Oakhill House (established 2009) looks more like something off a TV design show: wavy award-winning architecture; a fern-strewn courtyard complete with decking and modern sculptures; its own gym, art studio and huge windows looking out onto thirty acres of grounds. And most of the time I hated it.

There were two kinds of kids at Oakhill House: the ones who were desperate to avoid being discharged; and the ones, like me, who were desperate to get out. All I wanted was for my MTD – the multi-disciplinary team – to release me back into the wild. And every night I'd make a pact with myself that I was going to say and do all the right things. Unfortunately it doesn't work like that.

So why have I come back? What strange logic has drawn me to the scene of my darkest nightmares? The answer's simple. This is where it all started to make sense.

And one place was special: a secret place, somewhere only the two of us knew about. I figure that if I can just get back to it, I might feel better.

But the night staff are arriving for the changeover in a procession of clapped-out cars (the Mercedes C-Class saloon probably belongs to the consultant). No matter how unlikely it is, I can't run the risk of being recognised. So I hide in the trees, waiting for my chance. And when the last of the smokers drifts back inside for dinner, I shoot across the car park and down the hill, hugging the shadows in case the new inmates of the asylum think I'm a burglar and call security.

Waiting for me at the bottom is a row of derelict Portakabins, where yesterday's lunatics assembled transistor radios or tended tomato plants. Slowly decaying, their shattered windows an aching mouthful of jagged teeth, it's about time the wrecking ball put them out of their misery. I crunch across the broken glass, craning my neck backwards and squinting up.

And there it is, piercing the night sky like a three-hundred-foot penis: the old water tower. *Erected by direction of the Asylum Visiting Committee to secure a better provision in case of fire.* It looks like the kind of place a Disney knight would rescue a Disney princess from, with fake battlements and ivy climbing the wall.

The Disney knight would probably have hauled himself up the princess's hair extensions. But if he'd taken the trouble to do his research he would have found the rusty iron staircase at the back.

Last time I'd needed a bunk-up. I'm a lot taller now, so getting one foot up between the spiky green railings and launching myself over isn't nearly as impossible as it once seemed. Ducking under the *DANGER: KEEP OUT* sign, I pull up the collar of the old man's raincoat and start climbing.

Last time it was the middle of summer. Tonight it's wet, cold and slippery, and the wind's whistling around my mud-stained ankles. I stick close to the wall, like a cartoon bank robber on the run, already wishing I'd taken up jogging like Dad suggested. Because by the time I step out onto the roof, I can hardly breathe.

Weeds are sprouting up everywhere and I'm sure that crack wasn't there before. I nestle down in our favourite spot by the back wall, pulling my knees up to my chest and trying to look on the bright side. But you know what? I'm not feeling too great. Not surprising really, because I've started thinking about school.

He's bound to have told them. The Chinese whispers will have whizzed down the corridors and be all over Facebook by now. How can I go back there if everyone knows? What's the point if it's just like before?

Maybe this will make me feel better. There's no wall at the front of the water tower, just a row of fake battlements with two-metre gaps between them and a sheer drop onto the spiky railings below.

I walk towards the precipice, staring into the half-light. On a clear day you can see forever, but with the stars dimmed behind a cloudy curtain of rain, I can only make out the dark outline of the woods and a twinkly crocodile of cars heading home.

Half a metre from the edge I start feeling better. And I'm seriously thinking about taking the next step, when a familiar voice stops me dead in my tracks.

'I thought I'd find you up here.'

34

LAB RATS

H always insisted that he wasn't an emo. He was just a twelve-year-old boy who liked to dye his hair and wear make-up. 'Who wants to be like everyone else?' he said, talking to his trainers as usual. 'You've got to dare to be different.'

A lot of them came out with that kind of crap in group discussion sessions, 'inspirational' stuff they'd picked up on Facebook and trotted out for the benefit of their treatment teams. So it wasn't his taste in advertising slogans that we bonded over, it was gambling and drugs.

The pool table in the recreation room was usually dominated by the older kids. Maybe there was a fight that night or some other Oakhill House psychodrama, because for once the table was free. I knew we shared the same key worker, so it was just possible he'd put him up to it, but it was a major surprise when the kid with jet-black hair and a soft squeaky voice challenged me to a game.

H was an old hand. I'd only been there a week; I was still terrified that I was surrounded by nutters. And perhaps if I'd noticed some of his more bizarre behaviours (always touching things right in the middle, only taking a pee at five, ten, twenty-five or fifty-five minutes past the hour) I would have rushed back to my little room with the blindingly white walls. But there was something so unthreatening about his refusal to make eye contact that – although I'd never played before – I said I'd 'give it a shot'.

'Is that supposed to be a joke?' he said, chalking his cue fifteen times.

'No,' I replied.

And after he'd shown me the basics, we had a bet on how many colours I'd have left, and he fleeced me of my chocolate rations.

Like half the others at Oakhill House, we were both on twenty milligrams of Prozac: a green and white capsule that I struggled to swallow every morning. So while we played, we talked drugs, checking off side-effects like a shopping list.

'Dry mouth?'

'Uh-huh.'

'Feel sick the whole time?'

'But can't puke either?'

'Yeah. (Nice shot.)'

'Feel like a zombie. But not in a good way?'

'Yeah, or like an animal they're experimenting on.'

'Lab rats, that's what we are.'

'How about dreams where you want to kill somebody?'

I had those *before* I started taking Prozac, but I wasn't going to tell H that. 'Sometimes, yeah.'

'But there's one good thing about it.'

'What's that then?'

'At least it makes you feel better.'

It wasn't one of those intense friendships that sometimes developed in there, but after the game of pool we'd often find ourselves sitting together down in the dining room while they tortured the anorexics with a full-fat yoghurt, or sharing a nervous smile when someone had a public meltdown. We didn't talk much. Both of us liked fast cars, but I'd never heard of half the bands he was into, and he certainly wasn't interested in designer clothes.

Of course, the main thing we had in common was depression, although H had admitted himself to Oakhill House voluntarily, whereas after threatening the food-tech teacher with an electric mixer, they'd left me with no choice.

It was the middle of August so there were no classes, just a drug-dulled tedium of art therapy, African drumming lessons and weekly meetings with your treatment team. So it was a real release when your key worker decided you were well enough to walk in the grounds. At first we just dawdled over to the hospital shop together, but after a while H wanted to explore.

It was H who decided we should climb the water tower, catapulting me over the railings and racing up the iron staircase because he was desperate to see how many steps there were. And for a few weeks we sat on the roof counting clouds. Well, H did – I lay back and listened. In between counting, he'd let slip the occasional detail about his past, and gradually I pieced together his backstory:

After several months of CBT and exposure therapy he was finally getting it under control. At its worst, he could barely leave the house. But it had all started with a tuna sandwich.

Two weeks after his dad went off with the kitchen designer H had this terrible premonition his mum was going to die. That's when the 'magical thinking' kicked in. At least they call it magical; I don't see it myself. H decided that if he chewed every mouthful of his sandwich thirty-two times, he could keep his mum alive. And after it worked, he did the same thing at every meal. But it didn't stop there. His list of rituals grew longer by the second: checking every electrical appliance eight times before he went to bed (if they weren't switched off his mum faced certain cremation); changing his computer password twice daily; only typing with his left hand. And then there was the obsessive washing: four times an hour with antibacterial gel and a scrubbing brush. He told his mum it was to protect her from bubonic plague. That's when they knew he needed help.

It made for interesting listening. So I was happy to sit back and relax. But then, one afternoon, H started asking questions.

'So what's *your* problem then? I know you're angry about something, but what is it?'

He was the first person I ever told.

And I'll always remember his reaction: not horror or nervous laughter even, just a casual shrug and a few words of encouragement. 'It's all right, I understand. Everyone deserves a second chance.'

Back then I was glad I'd told him. From where I'm standing now, it feels like the worst mistake I ever made.

Sometimes H wanted to play 'chicken', seeing how close to the edge we could get. It seemed strange for someone who was frightened of practically everything, but he said it made him feel alive.

It made me feel better too, although it certainly wasn't because I felt alive, quite the opposite in fact. You see, I always figured that if things got too much for me I'd be able to jump.

35

SOMEWHERE ONLY WE KNOW
(PART TWO)

'I think you'd better come away from there,' says Harry. 'You're making me nervous.'

'Supposing I don't want to?'

'Come on, Lauren. You could really hurt yourself.'

'I thought that was the whole point.'

'It's so dangerous, especially in all this rain.'

'You used to enjoy it,' I say, turning shakily to face him. 'Why don't you have a try?'

'Stop it,' he says, dropping his crash helmet and edging towards me. 'It was a stupid game. I was ill. You know that – we both were.'

'Oh, so you know who I am then?'

'Of course I do. I've known for a long time.' (Right.) 'It took me a while. But there was something really familiar about you. And then when you started asking all those questions, I gradually worked out why.'

'No shit, Sherlock.'

'Just come here, Lauren, *please*. Then we can talk about it.'

'Why didn't you say anything? Why did you pretend you didn't know me?'

'Why do you think?' he says, taking another step towards me, his arm outstretched.

'You tell me, H.'

'Don't call me that.'

'Yeah, all right, keep your hair on.'

'Please, Lauren. You're frightening me.'

'You haven't answered my question yet. If you knew who I was, why didn't you say?'

'I've never told anyone at school about my . . . I didn't want them finding out I'd been in Oakhill House. You know what people are like,' says Harry. 'And you obviously didn't want to talk about it either, so I just kept quiet.'

'Yes but —'

'We've both changed so much since then. It didn't seem fair.' His outstretched arm begins to shake. 'Please, Lauren, just come away from the edge.'

'Why should I?'

'Because I'm begging you.'

Harry looks so desperate that I grab hold of his hand.

He wraps his arms round me, like a human straitjacket, and I drink in the reassuring combination of sweat, machine oil and Calvin Klein. 'Don't ever do that to me again. You scared me to death.' Eventually he lets go. 'What's that you're wearing anyway?'

'I got it from the woman I hitched a ride with.'

'You didn't hitch, did you? You do know how stupid that was?'

'You're telling me. She was driving a Peugeot 107.'

Harry smiles. 'So you're still into cars then?'

'Yeah, course, why shouldn't I be?'

He takes a collapsible umbrella from his coat pocket, magicking it into life, like a schoolboy Mary Poppins. 'Want to sit down for a bit?'

'Yeah, why not?'

And without thinking, we take our place against the back wall, peering through the clouds at the smudgy stars.

'You're not counting them, are you, Harry?'

'No,' he says, putting his arm round me. 'I'm just thinking how beautiful they are.'

'That's good then,' I say, resting my head on his shoulder. 'So how have you been?'

'Yeah, good. Most days. I still get a bit down sometimes, but I know how to handle it now.'

'Good.'

'I was pretty confused when I realised who you were though. That's why I kept my distance for a bit. I thought for a while it might, you know, set me off again. But even before we started . . . getting closer, I always tried to look out for you.'

I pull away from him, suddenly remembering how angry I am. 'Look out for me? Is that what you call it?'

'I still don't understand why you walked out of school, Lauren. I could see you were losing it, but why?'

'Let's cut the crap, shall we? I'm talking about all those "presents" you sent me.'

'What presents?'

I pull out the screwed-up Wallace and Gromit card. '"*Why don't you tell them what you did to Luke?*" Don't pretend you didn't write it, Harry. Who else could have done it?'

He takes out his phone and shines it on the message. 'Well, it wasn't me. I would *never* try and mess with your head like that.'

'Yeah, right.'

'Oh come on. Do you honestly think I'd start playing mind games after everything you've been through? I know what it's like, Lauren. I could never do that to you.' He taps out a rhythm on my shoulder. Anyway, that's not the only reason. I think I —'

'What?'

'Nothing, I — Look, I swear it wasn't me, okay?'

'Fine, I believe you. But then who was it? No one else knows.'

'What about the teachers?'

'A couple of them, but they'd never say anything.'

'Supposing someone let it slip by accident? Or what if it was a kid from your old school?'

'They don't know where I am. At least I don't think so. But it's just the kind of thing those bastards would do.'

Harry squeezes my shoulder. 'What happened there anyway?'

'It was just *vile*. I thought because they'd known me before they'd at least treat me with a bit of respect. I even created my own YouTube channel to try and explain it to them. But they couldn't leave me alone. And the girls were worse than the boys. Sometimes it was physical, and not a PE lesson went by when I didn't have my kit stolen. But most of the time it was just a never-ending stream of nastiness on the internet.

'And then this boy in my year, Ben, started showing an interest in me. I thought he was a nice guy. So when he asked if I wanted to catch a movie, I thought I might be getting somewhere. But it was all a big set-up. Half my tutor group turned up. Ben went to sit with them, and they pelted me with popcorn from the back row.

'I just couldn't take it any more. So when me and Mum got back from the States, we all decided to make a fresh start and move to a place where nobody knew about me. But then you came along, Harry.'

'So that's what you meant about leading you on. You think I'm going to turn out like that Ben guy.'

'I don't know . . . aren't you?'

'Of course not. That would *never* happen.'

'Why?'

'Because I – Because I really, *really* like you, Lauren.'

'And it doesn't feel weird or anything?'

'Well, let's find out, shall we?'

I close my eyes and enjoy the 'experiment' – twice.

'Not weird at all,' says Harry. 'Pretty amazing, in fact.'

He's right, the kiss was amazing. But it still doesn't solve anything. 'So what do I do now?'

'What do you mean?' says Harry.

'Well, I can't go back to school, can I?'

'Why not?'

'I just can't.'

'But you've come so far, Lauren. Are you really going to throw it away because some idiot can't handle it?'

'What if they've told everyone?'

'Well, they haven't said anything so far.'

'I just don't think I can face it.'

'Yes you can, because you won't be on your own any more. I'll tell them everything you've been through; how I knew you from before.'

'I thought you didn't want anyone to know.'

'Why should I be ashamed of it? And why should you? You're not going to give up now, are you?'

'I don't know – maybe.'

'Come on, let's go down, shall we? I know someone who'd be really pleased to see you. Why don't you pop in and say hi while I park my bike?'

36

BIG MOE

And after I've told him everything, Big Moe orders me a taxi on his brand-new phone.

'Should be about ten minutes, Lauren.'

'Thanks, Moe.'

'I don't think I'll ever get used to this thing. I preferred the other one. Christ knows where I lost it – must be getting old.'

I warm my bum on the radiator, sipping sickly-sweet tea from a *World's Best Nurse* mug. 'I thought you weren't talking to me or something.'

'You know I'd never do that.'

'No, I know. I was just feeling a bit . . . fragile.'

'It's so good to see you, Lauren. And you're looking great.'

'I look like shit.'

'Aye, well, you've been out in the rain, haven't you? But I'm sure you scrub up nice when you want to.'

Big M was the second person I told. If it wasn't for

my amazing key worker, I'd never have had the courage to tell Mum and Dad.

'It's good to see you too, Moe.'

'Get away with you, you'll make me cry.'

'So you'll talk to my mum then?'

'I'll call her when you're on your way. I'm sure she'll have calmed down a bit now she knows you're safe.'

'And you'll tell her it's no big deal and she doesn't need to worry?'

'She's your mum, Lauren. It's her job.'

'I wish she'd take a holiday now and then.'

Big Moe taps confusedly on his touchscreen. 'So, what are you going to do now your little secret's out?'

Typical Big Moe, making a joke of it. 'I don't know,' I say. 'Harry thinks I should just get on with it.'

Big Moe laughs. 'Now that's something I never saw coming – young Harry handing out advice.'

'He's done really well, Moe. You should see him at school.'

'I bet you nearly had a heart attack when *he* walked into the classroom.'

'It was the school field actually. And he's changed his hair and everything.'

But now Moe can see for himself. Harry's standing in the doorway with a huge smile on his face. 'Reception buzzed me through, Moe. They said it was all right to pop down and say hello.'

Big Moe roars with delighted laughter. 'Oh dear God, it's not, is it? Well, look at you.'

'Hi, Moe.'

'Well, you know what they say. There's only one way to make an elephant laugh.'

And we all join in with the punchline: 'Tell him a gorilla joke!'

Moe spots Harry's crash helmet. 'Don't tell me they're letting you out on the roads?'

'It's only a moped,' says Harry. 'I can't do more than thirty miles an hour. It took me ages to get here.'

'Thank God for that,' says Big Moe. 'You and wee Luke were right little speed freaks.'

A cold blast from the past fills Moe's stuffy office with the temporary sound of silence. The shouting in the corridor gets louder.

'So, anyway, how have you been, Moe?' says Harry.

'Oh, you know, getting older, losing my phone . . . putting my foot in it as usual. What about you, Harry? Lauren says you're doing good.'

'Well, you know, most of the time.' He taps absentmindedly on his crash helmet. 'I've still got my Happy Box.'

And if I didn't know Moe better, I'd swear there were tears in his eyes. 'Well, this is great. I never thought I'd see you guys together again.'

But the noise in the corridor is getting harder to ignore and Big Moe springs into action. He looked pretty short when I was twelve years old; standing next to him now makes me feel like a giant.

'Sorry, got to go. No rest for the wicked and all that.'

He takes another look at Harry's crash helmet. 'You will be careful on that thing, won't you, Harry?'

'Don't worry, Moe, he'll be fine. If he went any slower he'd be going backwards.'

'At least I'll be getting home tonight,' Harry said, smiling. 'What are you going to do, Lauren – walk?'

'Walk! Not bloody likely. I am going in a taxi.'

Dad pays the taxi driver, while Mum whisks me up to my room. Tilda's sitting at the top of the stairs crying.

'What happened?' she says, a mouse's tail of mascara on her cheek.

'Nothing really, I just lost it for a bit.'

'Why did you even go there?'

'I don't know. I thought it might make me feel better.'

'So is it true that Harry was in Oakhill House too?'

'Yes.'

'And do you think —'

But Mum's obviously desperate to get me alone. She pushes me into my bedroom and closes the door behind us.

'So tell me what happened.'

'Didn't Big Moe explain?'

'Yes he did, Lauren. But I want to hear it from you.'

'Well, I —'

'And where did you get that coat?'

'Someone gave it to me.'

'What?'

210

'It's okay, Mum. I hitched a lift with this lady and she practically insisted.'

'Hitch-hiking. My God, you didn't, did you?'

'It was fine, honest. Look, I know you were worried and everything, but nothing happened. I just —'

'I don't even want to think about it right now. You're safe and that's the main thing. Why don't you have a nice bath and go to bed?'

'But, Mum, I want to tell you about —'

'Dad's going to take tomorrow morning off work. We can talk about it then.'

'What about school?'

'Well, you can't go back, can you?'

And as soon as I say it, I know it's what I want. 'Of course I can. It's the fashion show tomorrow. I need to be there first thing to check my outfits.'

'I'm sorry, darling, you're not thinking straight. We wondered about home schooling for a bit – you were quite keen on the idea once.'

'No way.'

'But if someone at school knows about you, you've got no choice.'

'I *do* have a choice, Mum. That's the whole point. And I'm not on my own any more. If someone's got something to say to me, they can say it to my face.'

37

SHOWTIME

A mountain of lost property lies mouldering in the corner. I pace the sweaty equipment store in the yellow beach dress. Despite the massive butterflies flapping their wings in my stomach, all I want to do now is get on with it.

'It's the St Thomas's wedding of the year,' says Harry, his crudely amplified voice echoing around the sports hall. 'The pageboys are in blue suits with ivory waistcoats and pink cravats . . .'

A few wolf whistles.

'. . . and the bridesmaids look simply gorgeous in their beaded-bodice pleat dresses from Dressed to Kill in East Street. And, by the way, Magda has asked me to remind you there's a five per cent discount if you mention St Thomas's to the manager.'

A sarcastic 'Oooeeeooo.'

'And here they are, the happy couple.'

It's the loudest cheer of the night, by about a million decibels.

'The bride's ivory ball gown comes courtesy of Briding My Time, and the groom's grey morning suit is available at all branches of Moss Bros.'

The crowd goes absolutely mental.

Thirty ear-splitting seconds later, my blushing form tutor floats into the equipment store. 'The atmosphere out there's amazing,' says Miss Hoolyhan. 'Did you hear the reception we got?'

'I told you you would.'

'I think even Colin . . . I mean, Mr Catchpole, enjoyed it.'

'Brilliant.'

'And the photos of Westminster Abbey were perfect.'

'Thanks, miss.'

'I think I'll watch the rest from backstage. Don't worry, I haven't forgotten your quick change.'

'Would you like me to help you out of that dress first, miss?'

'Do you know, I think I'll keep it on for a bit.' She runs a loving hand across the intricate tapework. 'Not nervous, are you, Lauren?'

'No, miss.'

'Well, you certainly don't need to be, because you look lovely. Anyway, good luck, and I'll see you on the catwalk!'

Harry introduces the Year Seven recycling project.

Time for a final check in the mirror; just this track and I'm on. Luckily the yellow beach dress looks pretty stunning (though I say it myself) and the Great Wall of Eczema, which only this morning was clearly visible from outer space, has all but vanished. But I was lying about not being nervous. I'm petrified. The thought that someone out there knows about me is doing my head in.

I collapse onto the blue PE mats, acupressuring my temples with my index fingers and trying to get it together. But the music's so loud I can hardly hear myself think; so loud that at first I don't recognise her.

'Mind if I come in?'

'Eh?'

'I just wanted to —'

'Oh it's you. Are the stomach cramps better then? I thought you weren't coming.'

'I wasn't.'

She's still in school uniform. She must have rushed up here at the last minute.

'Well, I'm really glad you did.'

Talk about role reversal. For the second time in twenty-four hours, it looks like Tilda's the one who's been crying.

'There's something I—'

But she can't get the words out.

'What's the matter, Tilds? Are you okay?'

She sits beside me, her shoulders trembling. 'There's something I need to tell you.'

'I'm on in a minute. Can it wait?'

'Not really, no.'

She looks so awful. 'This isn't about a boy, is it?'

'Kind of.'

214

'Then I probably won't be much help. But you can give it a try if you want.'

Silence, apart from three hundred screaming St Thomas's kids and their even rowdier parents.

And when Tilda does speak, it doesn't make sense. 'It was me.'

'What?'

'I said it was me.'

'Eh?'

'It was me that sent you all that . . . stuff.'

At first I think I haven't heard her right. 'What are you talking about, Tilds?'

'The dinosaur . . . Paddington Bear with the knife in his back.'

It takes me a while to process what she's saying.

'Why would you do that?'

'Because I was angry with you; I wanted to make you suffer.'

'But why? I thought you and me were okay again?' I'm still numb; still shocked.

Tilda hates Coldplay. But that's not why she's struggling to get the words out. 'You have no idea what it's like – being your sister. What they did to you was terrible. But I had it nearly as bad you know: all the crap on Facebook; jokers lining up in the playground to have a pop at me; graffiti on practically everything I owned. And *I* hadn't even done anything. Then when you ran off to the States with Mum because you couldn't hack it any more, I'm still stuck there having the piss ripped out of me.'

My own sister. I don't believe it.

'At least I had a few friends that stuck by me. The next thing I know we're moving miles away and I'm not allowed to see them any more.'

'We all agreed it was for the best.'

Tilda nods. 'Yeah, and maybe it would have been if you'd done what you said and kept your head down. But we'd only been here two minutes and you were signing up for sodding fashion shows. It was almost like you wanted someone to find out.'

'No, I was just —'

'I thought if I frightened you enough, you wouldn't do it.'

'I nearly didn't.'

'But it stopped being about that when you started seeing Harry. I was so angry, especially after what happened last time.' She sniffs up a gobbet of snot. 'It felt like you were the only one that Mum and Dad cared about. I just wanted to hurt you.'

'How could you even *think* like that?'

'I know. When I saw you last night, I realised what a total bitch I'd been, that I was just as bad as the rest of them. No, *worse* – your own sister making your life a misery. You didn't deserve that.'

'No, I didn't.' The numbness is wearing off, I'm starting to feel anger bubble up.

'I've missed you . . . Lauren.'

It stops me in my tracks. I can hardly believe my ears. That's the first time she's used my real name. 'Okay, okay I get it. At least I *kind* of get it. So I'm going to ask you this one more time, Tilda. Do you really think we can make this sister thing work?'

'Yeah,' she says, wiping her nose on her school jacket. 'I reckon we can.'

And I should probably leave it there, but there's one more question I have to ask. 'What did it all mean, anyway – Paddington Bear and the rest of them?'

'Think about it,' says Tilda.

Deep down I knew all along. But it's as if it suddenly dawns on me. 'Oh. Yeah . . . right. They were . . . Luke's favourite toys, weren't they?'

And for the briefest moment, Tilda's face goes into mourning. 'I miss *him* too,' she says.

But the familiar guitar riff with the insistent bassline means only one thing. I jump up from the PE mats and race to the door. 'That's my cue, Tilds. I'll see you in a minute.'

'No, wait,' she says, racing after me and grabbing hold of my hand. 'There's something else.'

'Look, I can't deal with this right now, Tilda. I've gotta go.'

'No, Lauren, you can't.'

'Haven't you done enough?' I say, grabbing my hand back and pushing angrily past her. 'You've made a pretty good job of messing with my head, but you are *not* going to stop me walking down that runway to my favourite song.'

'You don't understand, I —'

But I can't hear her. The Beatles classic 1969 hit single, 'Get Back' is filling the sports hall. And the atmosphere backstage is electric. Excited Year Sevens in their bin-liner and cornflake-packet ensembles high-five me as they run giggling towards their changing area, Miss Hoolyhan mouths a smiley 'good luck', and even Katherine looks up from her laptop to offer me an ironic two-fingered peace sign.

I take my place at the foot of the catwalk alongside a glistening figure in swimming trunks.

'All right, Dizzy?' says Conor Corcoran. 'You look a bit—'

'I'm fine,' I snap. 'In fact, I couldn't be better, Conor. But what about you? What have you done to yourself?'

'Well, you've got to oil up, haven't you? Tell you what, babe, maybe later on you could rub it in for me.'

'In your dreams.'

When the chorus comes in, we start walking.

And I'm so up for it. At least now Tilda's told me everything, I know my secret's still safe. I am *not* going to let her ruin the whole night for me.

'Conor is wearing black floral swimming shorts with a hidden tie string – let's hope he doesn't get sand kicked in his face. And the lovely Lauren is wearing a lace-panel yellow sundress – perfect for those lazy summer days.'

It feels fantastic, strutting down the runway to my favourite song. The audience seem to be loving it too, screaming their approval and stamping their feet. Even Dad's smiling. And with Harry at the side of the stage to share the moment with me, it couldn't be more perfect.

But when I get to the front and start posing, something strange happens.

The screaming stops, and then turns to a feverish murmur. A second later the music cuts out. That's when I see the kids in the third row pointing, and I half wonder if Conor Corcoran is doing something inappropriate behind my back. But as soon as I turn round, it all becomes clear.

'Jesus . . . no.'

The whispering stops. An eerie quiet fills the sports hall.

There on the screen at the back of the catwalk are three life-sized images. The first is a nine-year-old boy in an Arsenal football shirt, the second a screenshot from a YouTube video of an awkward teenager in a flowery blouse with too much make-up and the hint of a moustache, and the third is a sixteen-year-old girl on her first day at St Thomas's, posing unwillingly for her mum's iPhone next to a single hand, the rest of whose body has been brutally amputated.

So far so random.

Except there's probably something else I should tell you.

All three photographs are of me.

But just in case someone out there doesn't get it, the caption underneath reads:

HOW LUKE BECAME LAUREN

38

WHO I AM

I stare into the audience. Every eye in the sports hall stares back at me.

'Well, I don't know what that's all about,' says the flustered compere. 'We seem to have had a small technical hitch. But if you just —'

'It's okay, Harry,' I say, grabbing his microphone. 'I'll take it from here.'

'You don't have to do this you know,' he whispers, grasping my hand and refusing to let go.

What choice do I have? If I'm ever going to be the person I want to be, it's now or never. 'That's okay, Harry. I know what I have to do.'

Word must have filtered through backstage, because by now Magda, Izzy and the rest of the models are lining the catwalk, Katherine and Grunt have deserted their post at the sound desk and Miss Hoolyhan and Mr Catchpole stand grim-faced by the fire exit, like a nearly married couple, upstaged by a last-minute gatecrasher with secrets from their past.

I scour the audience for a friendly face. She really is the most incredible woman, because instead of tears or hysteria, she smiles encouragingly, like the parent of that innkeeper who forgot his lines in the Nativity play. And, like twelve Christmases ago, if I focus on Mum I might just be able to get through it.

'Have you ever seen one of those movies where someone wakes up in the wrong body? Well, it happened to me for real.'

How can silence get even quieter? But somehow it does.

'I always knew I was a girl, even when I was little. It wasn't exactly rocket science. My favourite game was dressing up in my sister's Snow White outfit and playing princesses. But there was one big problem. I was born a boy and my parents called me Luke.'

There's a nervous giggle from the front row. It's the boy who claims to read fiction for pleasure.

'That's me in my Arsenal kit. Dad thought I was going to be the next Thierry Henry. Sorry, Dad.'

Dad half smiles, half tries to disappear.

'I didn't tell anyone because . . . well, because I thought it might go away. It didn't, of course. I couldn't play princesses any more, but when everyone was out, I used to put on Mum's clothes and experiment with her make-up. And by the age of twelve I was so angry about having to keep it a secret that I ended up in the psych ward.

222

That's where I first told someone.' I turn to Harry. He squeezes my hand and nods. 'And once I'd told him, I felt much better.'

Right now, I'm not sure how I feel. At least no one's walked out yet.

'But that was just the beginning. Telling my family was the hardest thing I've ever done. And they were amazing – especially Mum. She even gave up work so she could drive me to London for my appointments. I still feel bad about it. Because it takes forever, convincing the "experts" about something you've known all your life. So I was nearly fifteen by the time I got my diagnosis.'

Tilda's standing by the wall bars still crying. Half of me can hardly bear to look at her; the other half wants to give her a big hug.

'Then last summer, I got the go ahead to start transitioning, to start my life as a woman, to begin becoming Lauren. That holiday was probably the happiest six weeks of my life. At last I could be the person I wanted to be, the person I always knew I was.

'But I made the mistake of thinking that everyone else would be happy for me too. When I went back to my old school as Lauren, they just couldn't cope. That was probably the *worst* time of my life. And if Mum and Dad hadn't been so brilliant, I think I would have . . .'

I take a deep breath. I am *not* going to cry. I am *not* bloody going to cry.

'In the end, Mum took me to a gender therapist in the

States who started me on hormone blockers and oestrogen. And after a while, I felt more confident about "passing".

'That's how I ended up here at St Thomas's. It was the new start I'd always dreamed of; where I could just be Lauren for a change and no one knew about my past.'

I glance back at my nine-year-old self. 'But I guess the little slide show has blown it. So there's one more thing I want to say to you.'

A bead of sweat sets off from my armpit. If this back-fires on me, it's game over.

'I can't live a lie any more. But I've put my family through enough already. So if anyone's got a problem with me, all you have to do is say something now and I'll never come back.'

Silence.

Harry leans across and kisses me on the cheek.

More silence.

And then the sound of footsteps as Katherine jumps onto the catwalk and wraps her arms round me in a most un-Katherine like way. 'I take back what I said about you,' she whispers. 'You're incredible. And I'm sorry about the photos. Someone must have messed about with them. I should have checked.'

Next to step forward is the oiled-up swimmer – which is probably the last thing I need. Because if anyone's going to mess this up for me it's Conor Corcoran.

'So what's the big deal?' he says, standing shoulder to shoulder with me and eyeballing the crowd. 'We're all with you, Lauren. This is the twenty-first century, you know.'

And pretty soon I'm joined onstage by some excited Year Sevens (still keen to high-five me despite the revelations); guys in tuxedos and girls in their prom dresses, pageboys and bridesmaids; Mrs Gough the art teacher who's been helping backstage; some Year Tens in their winter outfits; the boy who claims to read fiction for pleasure; half the netball team in Lycra; Magda, Izzy and all the dressers and an 'emotional' Miss Hoolyhan.

Only Tilda hangs back, standing alone at the side of the stage, like the last person to be picked for netball. I'm still pretty furious with her, but I really need my sister to be part of this, so I smile and beckon her over.

Tilda pushes her way through my crowd of supporters, whispering, 'Sorry, Lauren,' as we fall into a tearful embrace.

But it's only when health and safety becomes an issue that the ageing groom with the droopy moustache steps onto the catwalk and takes charge of the microphone.

'Thank you, Lauren, that was most . . . interesting,' says Mr Catchpole, brushing away a blob of moisture that can't possibly be a tear. 'Sometimes as a teacher you learn more from your pupils than you ever thought possible. As most of you know, courage and tolerance are two of our school community's key values. I think we've seen excellent examples of both of them tonight.'

He pulls a crumpled Tesco bag from his morning suit.

'Now before we continue, perhaps this is a good time

to draw the raffle. The prizes this evening include two tickets for the Wetlands Centre, a twenty-pound spa voucher and an iPod Shuffle. The PTA has also donated a . . .'

39

EIGHT MONTHS LATER

It took me a while to forgive Tilda for sabotaging the fashion show. And even longer to come to the conclusion that (screwed up though it was), in a way, she'd actually done me a favour. After all, if it hadn't been for her, I might never have had the chance to tell everyone the truth about myself.

I'm not saying it's been easy – the sister thing, I mean; we've both had to work hard at rebuilding our relationship. But at least we never stopped talking about it, and these days I honestly reckon we're closer than ever.

'Come on, Lauren,' she says, pointing her iPad at me. 'Grandma wants to see your prom dress.'

We bought her a laptop for her eighty-fifth birthday, and amazingly, she can't get enough of it.

'Hi, Grandma,' I say, waving at the twinkly-eyed octogenarian on the screen. 'What do you think?'

'You look lovely, Lauren,' she says, distorting a little

as she peers into her webcam. 'Make sure you put some photos on Facebook.'

'Yeah, will do.'

'So where's your friend then?' says Grandma. 'Come on, Katherine, give us a twirl.'

Katherine's gone to a lot of trouble for someone who's only going to the prom 'ironically'. All right, maybe she is dressed as a character from *Scooby-Doo*, but it took me two hours to straighten her hair and I'm quite sure the girl with glasses didn't wear make-up.

'Very nice dear,' says Grandma diplomatically. 'I'll Skype you tomorrow, Lauren, for all the gossip.'

'The car's arrived,' calls Dad. 'Come on, girls, you don't want to be late for the ball.'

But before we go I should probably tell you what happened after the fashion show. It wasn't quite the Hollywood ending I was hoping for. Miss Hoolyhan wouldn't say anything, but I know for a fact that a few worried parents phoned in the next morning about the changing arrangements for PE. Then there were the kids who took ridiculous amounts of pleasure from calling me 'the gender bender', a Facebook page that soon got taken down, and the girl with the purity ring who was keen to promote her dad's message that 'God doesn't make mistakes'.

But gradually, school got better. And after a while, I actually started to look forward to it. Mr Catchpole even asked Harry and me to talk to his PSHE groups about teenage mental health issues and how I'd coped with my transition.

We had some pretty interesting discussions. Although when it came to the Q & A sessions, two questions seemed to crop up with monotonous regularity.

And just for the record here are the answers:

1. Yes, I've still got one.
2. I don't know yet.

But I *do* know how lucky I am. What are a few nasty comments when you've got good friends? It's a small price to pay for truly being yourself. Because there are some places where being yourself comes with a prison sentence – or worse.

'Hurry up, Lauren,' calls Mum. 'George is here.'

Grunt is standing in the hallway with a bouquet of mixed vegetables, which he presents to Katherine.

'They're lovely,' she says, kissing him on the cheek and giving him a Scooby Snack.

Those two were made for each other.

'Okay, ladies,' says Grunt. 'Your carriage awaits.'

Mum, Dad and Tilda follow us out to the road to wave goodbye.

Now *that's* what I call a cool car: a classic VW Camper, with blue petals for hub caps and *The Mystery Machine* in big orange letters on the side. Velma and Shaggy take the front seat, and Grunt's dad, who's dressed as a chauffeur, slides open the back door so I can climb in next to my prom date.

There's one more thing I should probably tell you. I'm not seeing Harry any more. We're still close, and we hang out together all the time, but we both agreed that with our shared history we were probably better off as 'just friends'.

So anyway, you'd better meet my prom date. We've been going out for nearly six weeks now, and I have to say, things are looking good.

'Wow,' says Conor, handing me a single white rose. 'You look beautiful, babe.'

I was surprised too, but he kind of grew on me. He's funny and loyal and actually a really nice person once you get to know him. After all, I should know better than anyone that first appearances can sometimes be deceptive.

ABOUT THE AUTHOR

Simon Packham was a stand-up comedian and then an actor for twenty years before becoming a writer. He has published four previous books, including *Silenced*, which was shortlisted for several awards including the Leeds Book Award. Follow him at www.simonpackham.com or on Twitter: @baldambitions

PRESS

Thank you for choosing a Piccadilly Press book.

If you would like to know more about our authors, our books or if you'd just like to know what we're up to, you can find us online.

www.piccadillypress.co.uk

You can also find us on:

We hope to see you soon!